PRAISE FOR M

"This book makes *Cabin at the End of the World* by Paul Tremblay look like a cakewalk. This is THE MOST intense psychological horror you have ever read. Seriously. It makes *Out* by Natsuo Kirino look tame."

LIBRARY JOURNAL (*STARRED REVIEW*)

"Seidlinger pulls no punches in delivering gut-wrenching horror as he drives the novel to its bloody conclusion. Fans of Jack Ketchum and Samantha Kolesnik will want to check this out."

PUBLISHERS WEEKLY

"*Anybody Home?* is like nothing I've read before. Absolutely terrifying in its scope and clinically detached violence. I read this in a flurry. It's my first read of Seidlinger's work but it will not be my last."

ONLY THE DARKEST READS

"Harrowing and tremendously upsetting, *Anybody Home?* flips the home invasion genre on its head for a new generation of readers. I felt like I was reading something I shouldn't have been reading. You'll be checking your locks regularly after reading this nasty little morsel."

ERIC LAROCCA, AUTHOR OF *THINGS HAVE GOTTEN WORSE SINCE WE LAST SPOKE*

"A bone-chilling, immersive horror novel that explores fear, obsession, voyeurism, and senseless violence. Seidlinger takes an ax to the illusion of suburban safety. Unsettling, unflinching, and unforgettable. *Anybody Home?* is one of the most terrifying books I've ever read."

RACHEL HARRISON, AUTHOR
OF *CACKLE* AND *SUCH SHARP TEETH*

"Michael J. Seidlinger is a true innovator. The narrative shards of *Anybody Home?* cascade over the reader in a collage of troubling, sometimes half-seen images, and the wicked, insinuating, deeply unsettling voice weaves through the back of your mind and crouches in your dreams. A chilling and unforgettable book."

DAN CHAON, AUTHOR OF *SLEEPWALK*

"An ice cold, deadpan zeitgeist nightmare, Michael J. Seidlinger knows, and shows, that even in a lockdown moment, home is the most dangerous place of all. Watch out. Too late. They're watching you."

KATHY KOJA, AUTHOR OF *DARK FACTORY*

"*Anybody Home?* is *Natural Born Killers* for a generation that grew up on *Funny Games, The Purge,* and Twitter. An incisive commentary on how, in our culture, everything eventually gets mediatized—and a how-to guide to some of the darkest corners of that process, one that implicates you even as you read it."

BRIAN EVENSON, AUTHOR OF *SONG FOR THE UNRAVELING OF THE WORLD*

"In Michael J. Seidlinger's *Anybody Home?* your security alarm and cameras are positioned to betray you. Our invaders and our victims have been chosen carefully to perform in this meticulous, intoxicating, and brutal tale of home invasion."

"With this sinister and alluring story of home invasions, Michael Seidlinger has invented a new type of horror novel, one that simultaneously chronicles the characters' transgressions and the audience's reactions. It's a searing commentary on voyeurism and mass media, as well as a riff on Michael Haneke's *Funny Games* that outdoes the original. Read it with the doors locked."

"This addictive deconstruction of the home invasion is so thorough and chilling, Seidlinger may as well have slammed the door on the entire genre. But beyond the torture and violation, *Anybody Home?* is a nuanced study of the creative process, exploring what it takes to create art that truly resonates."

"In *Anybody Home?*, Michael J. Seidlinger so masterfully crafts an atmosphere of pure terror that it had me checking to make sure my front door was locked, for fear of home invaders—or maybe Seidlinger himself."

"*Anybody Home?* is a literal and metaphorical dissection of the nuclear family, executed with panache and filled with cutting insights. Seidlinger knows precisely how to make the reader complicit. These pages will bloody your hands, and it'll be a long time before the stains wash clean."

**BRIAN ASMAN, AUTHOR OF *MAN,
FUCK THIS HOUSE***

"Michael J. Seidlinger's *Anybody Home?* isn't just a deliriously terrifying novel, it's also a ransom note from our fame-obsessed id. It's an instruction manual from evil itself, and it's a mirror trick that puts you behind the eyes of a monster, only to realize the prey being stalked... is also you. This book is the best metafictional deconstruction of horror while also being straight-up effective horror novel since *American Psycho*."

**NAT CASSIDY, AUTHOR OF *MARY: AN
AWAKENING OF TERROR***

ANYBODY HOME?

MICHAEL J. SEIDLINGER

CL▲SH

Copyright © 2022 by Michael J. Seidlinger

Cover by Matthew Revert

matthewrevert.com

ISBN: 978-1-955904-09-4

Troy, NY

CLASH Books

clashbooks.com

PROLOGUE

According to the FBI, there are an estimated 1.7 million crimes reported every year. The quantity of reported crimes designated "home invasion" remains uncertain.

On the night of May 14th, 20XX, a family of four returned home from a day at a local amusement park. The events that took place over the following forty-eight hours are still not entirely known.

What you are about to witness is a sample of a factual record. If the sample is of any interest, the complete record can be made available to the studio upon request.

THE VICTIMS

#1
FATHER

#2
MOTHER

#3
DAUGHTER

#4
SON

ANYBODY HOME?

CHAPTER
ONE

WHAT ABOUT THE CAMERA? I'll tell you how it all falls into place. I'll tell you about the way you don't ever really have complete control over the situation. I'll go as far to tell you how long it takes to really wear one of them down. But you're the one that'll have to get used to the camera.

You're the one that'll have to frame the shot and make sure you get everything recorded. It's not going to be enough to leave behind a crime scene. You've got to think of it like a masterpiece, even if it doesn't get anywhere close. Think of everything like it'll be later picked apart, layer after layer.

Get a good brainstorm going. Figure out where it could all go right. Figure out where it'll all go wrong. Between the highs and lows, you'll see that it's a performance. The house targeted becomes the stage.

Do this and you've got it all made. Do that and you'll be able to satisfy the cults spun around the intimacies of the craft. The cults watch everything. The cults will show up to the premiere, buy it when it comes out on video, tell the world so you won't have to. They're all looking, wondering why one is any better than the rest. I'll tell you why so few rise to the top while the others sink and become just another crime statistic.

I can tell you everything.

But it'll be you that'll have to forget the camera's there.

Forget the camera because the camera's not going to forget you.

I've got to get this off my chest. You're dealing with other people's property, and more so, other people's homes, you have to get it straight before you don the mask, the role. You're probably asking—what the hell did you do to make it work?

Tell them right then and there, "Because we can."

You tell it to the victim's face, "You were home."

It's coincidental that they become the victims because it could have easily been anyone. Some say that everyone's capable of being at risk at some point in their home-owning, residence-renting existence.

The performance is nothing personal.

Fact:

You're always at risk.

It's what we—myself and one other invader who will never be named; no one is named, for the sake of your record, your future performance—liked the most. It's what got all the ideas forming, the gears of productivity and planning rolling. The realization that risk is always there. We liked that it was, inevitably, for the sake of the performance.

Nothing more. We do what we do because we can.

And we aren't the only ones entertained.

It had everything to do with entertainment.

Never forget the importance of entertainment.

What was it I said about the camera?

Exactly.

That's what I'm talking about.

Oh yeah, it was pretty wild, thinking about it now. The thing about this stuff—you don't think about it until it's all said and done. The whole thing signed on the dotted line. It's kind of like you become superstitious: Did I leave that one item I was supposed to leave? Did I send the text I was supposed to send? You become superstitious about the entire thing around the time the authorities start picking apart the layers. You watch it on the news. Hear about it on satellite radio. Keep tabs online, running traces, bookmarking various columns. You do all that, same as anyone else that's interested. Same as the investigators assigned to the case. Same as any potential studio representative looking for another great story. We're all on the edge of our seats, looking, watching, hearing, listening... senses strained for something to pop.

When it finally does pop, you don't have to worry as much.

It's actually a different kind of worry, now that I think about it.

You kind of worry that you won't really get to enjoy what everyone else is going to enjoy. You'll see the news reports, the writings about the act, people equally fascinated and disturbed about what you basically did for the performance, the performance that is now reaping its own kind of secondary, second stage performance. You'll see it all start to form as planned, and then you'll be caught up with whether or not you intended "this" to be like "that." Nothing's perfect, basically. That's what I'm trying to tell you.

I still look at the aftermath, the rollout, and wonder if one of the media outlets got a crucial bit of advice wrong.

Wonder if the cults devouring the performance are just digesting it—with each pass, becoming more diluted.

Someone's going to undo what we did.

Someone's going to one-up us.

It'll be another group of homes.

It'll be another meticulously planned performance.

It'll be received similarly, but this time it won't be like ours, where it was added to a list, made a marvel, only to be written down in a book, some creative nonfiction piece, made into a movie, based not on our performance but on that book, the literary analysis.

And then forgotten.

See, though—what we did hasn't been forgotten.

Because you're not the first to make contact, asking for advice, asking for something. It happens all the time. It's just that, in my mind and his, my partner in performance, the act is dead.

Any feeling we had for it, dead.

Long dead.

When I think about it now, really putting myself out there,

letting myself reminisce, I can almost feel the same rush, the same thrill, the same warmth that we received shortly afterward.

It was a different kind of celebrity.

We've got our names down on the books, in the FBI records.

I'm played by that actor that won an Oscar a few years back.

The reason we did what we did?

We did it for entertainment. We did it for enjoyment.

We did it for the attention.

We did it because we knew we could.

Nowadays, it's barely anything but something on the bookshelf, some archival print in the back of my mind.

But see, that's why you've got to make a dent.

Get it right the first time because you never know if you'll get a second chance.

Yeah, I know.

You want me to tell you about how we got the idea.

How we really got into it.

This is more about you, not me.

But I'll humor you. Promise me that you'll humor me when the time comes.

Just promise me, okay?

You'll know when it happens.

We started early, shortly before dawn. The camera was there even when we weren't. It started on the outer banks, and panned up and outward. We were dressed in white and made sure to keep everything clean. That's code for gloves. We started on the outskirts of a big lake. The name of the lake, like everything else, we leave unnamed. The authorities do the filling-in later. Give them too much and it's just another robbery or break-in and you don't want that.

But we had something in mind.

Daylight.

It almost never happens during the height of a new day.

It never happens during the week when vacationing families, looking to get away from the city, fill the houses lining the lake.

Camera shot wide across a paved road.

I can still picture SUVs and Escalades, newly washed sedans and sports-utility vans driving the speed limit, hulking with them bikes, boats, and other luxury items.

We had it right, which was a good sign when we knew.

We spotted the house on the far eastern bank, expecting it to be the one to begin what we would end up lengthening out across six houses before the end of the week.

Camera narrow in that driveway, the front gate opening and closing on its own. We walked around the back of the house. It was impressive, really it was.

The price on these houses is astronomical.

I couldn't imagine investing so much in something that is basically used only once or twice a year. These are getaway houses?

There was privilege in this community.

Many of the homeowners had small-to-medium empires of their own.

The more rural you get, the more of a performance it tends to be. That's something we learned in the months of planning before the final pull-off.

We learned that for all the tall gates and security systems, the guards and barking dogs at night, it's that level of silence that defines what rural can be.

The silence isn't security.

Just because those shrubs grow high, and the vines cover your windows, it doesn't mean that in the depths of the silence there isn't someone watching.

We watched.

We stepped inside these homes.

We took our time, learning their routines.

We weren't going for just another performance, you see.

We wanted to create a series of performances; this meant that we had to plan everything, every single invasion, as its own step. We spent at least eight months just on the setup, the planning. When it finally happened and he was in place, waiting for the first family to arrive, me in the backyard, awaiting the first cue, it was serenity. We almost saw the work, all that planning, play itself out, like a perfect take.

It felt like… like a perfect fit.

And then the family showed up.

There was a daughter—about eleven years of age—and the parents. They took their time getting situated, airing out the house, the wife wandering around out front, checking to see that the landscaper had successfully kept the flowers and other vegetation in shape. That freshly cut lawn wasn't the husband's doing.

We watched a crew arrive and tend to the house's upkeep.

Two actually. One of the employees wasn't as careful as the others. It's how we were able to get inside the house. It's easier than you think. It almost never has to come to actual break-ins or invasive lock picking.

Never learned how to pick a lock.

Few do. It's easier to figure out the source of the locked door than the lock itself.

By the time the daughter was indoors with the husband, who worked on fixing the power via the switchbox in the basement, the power we extricated an hour before their arrival, he knocked on the door.

He knocked on the door gently.

And I could tell from where I was, watching from a window to the wife's right.

She didn't see me but surely she saw him. He said what he was supposed to say, "Hello, I'm from the house down the road. We were wondering if you have any power? Ours seems to have gone out."

From there it was the wife calling to the husband, who then seemed relieved that it wasn't just their house that suffered from the power outage.

By then he was already inside. And so was I.

But I waited until he dropped a picture frame, the glass shattering, distracting the wife, who went into the room I just left, the kitchen, for a dustbin.

The husband tended to the broken frame.

He did a great job playing the pity case, apologizing profusely.

Then I was there, and they both wondered how I got in.

"We're friends, brothers actually."

See how I switched it up, making it unbelievable?

What better way to let them know that something's wrong than by acting strange. They had already welcomed my partner-in-performance in.

It was up to me to tend to the rest. I asked if they had a pet, maybe a dog.

I asked about their daughter.

By then, the daughter had been neutralized—tied up and taped—upstairs in her bedroom.

The wife called for the daughter.

The husband ran to fetch her.

The wife didn't take much to subdue.

She didn't even scream. She was all shivers—which I couldn't stand—so I got him to hold onto her while I followed the husband up the stairs.

Right around the time both the husband and the camera panned across a frightened daughter, a daughter that had pissed herself while alone in her room, the basics of the invasion had already begun. A quick strike to the back of the husband's head with a blunt object—in this case it was one end of the daughter's skateboard—and we could get to work. We tied them to their individual beds. We thought about what we should do. I remember looking around for a better angle, all the while wondering if our plan would really be enough. The husband regained consciousness and we got to talking. He proved to be an easy one to break apart. Talk about his life—career, hobbies, various flings he had on the side—and he'd begin to sob.

My partner-in-performance mentioned that his wife was attractive.

I joked about guessing her age.

I joked about whether she was in shape.

I wasn't joking when I asked the husband. And then the husband wouldn't tell me. We had to find out a different way. It turned into a game. I brought in the daughter, untied her so that she could run. The daughter forgot about the rope around her ankles.

"Poor thing. Now that didn't need to happen, did it?"

Plastic bag over and around the daughter's head got them playing. All throughout, we both looked to the situation, looked for something we could use. We needed to improvise because we were ahead of schedule.

Then I said the one thing that defined everything else:

"Let's play a game." With great effort, they played out various games in order to be untied, led back out in front of the house, and led to believe that they'd have to eat grass, if only to see that they aren't above being demeaned.

The daughter didn't make it though. I think we didn't let enough air in the bag. She suffocated on the fifth or sixth tightening of the bag around her neck. It was part of the game. Guess right and the daughter doesn't get hurt. This one moment became one of the more memorable characteristics of our performance.

It didn't end there either.

The games continued.

From the front yard, we saw the second family, as prototypical as the first, waving to each other, talking about dinner plans and yachts.

Shortly after finishing with the husband and wife, we followed the camera over to the next house, the next family. He asked about the power being out.

I wandered around back and waved to the husband with his young son, who looked approximately nine years old, where they were cleaning, maintaining their yacht.

I complimented them on the yacht's condition.

I told them I was a neighbor, using the same excuse: power-outage.

We played games mirroring the first family's set.

We made this one last a little longer before moving on. The wife being the last to go, sinking to the bottom of the lake like dead weight. We increased the games with each family until we had the sixth in turmoil—two teenage sons competing for their own lives while we watched. The games were simple. They started out like any little playground game but quickly mounted to be far more sinister for the camera. You tend to forget the camera. You see that it gets more on record than you ever could.

But the fact that it's there seems to satiate the cults. It seems to get as much of the picture as possible. Like, we didn't see how the sons of the sixth family ended their parents' lives in order to conceivably save theirs.

We didn't need to see that.

We left during the final couple strikes of the golf clubs on the cracked skull and shattered jaw of husband and wife, respectively.

By the time the authorities played their part, one son ran while the other chased after. It became their own deadly pursuit, a game based around the guilt they wouldn't be able to lose. The camera captured it long before the one son tackled the other to the ground, near a dock, and drove his thumbs into both sockets. With an injury like that, you don't just lose sight; you lose your life.

We weren't there though.

Camera captured what needed to be captured.

Later, it became just another piece of evidence, the footage for all to see. There would only be a few that would be in a position to profit on the record.

For most, the performance is as much about the payoff.

I'll tell you, though, in those last couple moments when our performance became more than the sum of each individual part, I could almost see it all—everything—for what it really was. I could see the various roles and the various emotions; I could see the authorities getting the call, coming the crime scene, marking up each house for their inevitable burial. I could see the effect of the events on the private community, causing a drop in property values and a rise in paranoia. I could see popular culture wrapping its mind around the performance. I could see borderline success long before we got an offer. I could see the annals of privacy and personal space shifting and contorting to welcome in a world realer than real. I could see the cults and their members clamoring over the uncensored footage. I could see them going through, like armchair investigators, long before the edited, commercialized version ever makes it onto the screen. I could see the trail of evidence slowly reaching us. I could see my own concern, worry mounting, if only because it would be more dramatic for it to end with our identities being revealed. Yet, like any other successful performance, we are deemed "invaders."

I was invader #1 and my partner-in-performance was invader #2.

Without names established they couldn't trace back our identities. Without fingerprints or true faces on footage—our likenesses little more than blurred pixels—the authorities couldn't get any closer than recovering the evidence and initial plan for invasion. It was an invasion and it invaded the collective senses. I could see success in all its conceptual glory. And it is beautiful. You know it is, otherwise you wouldn't be listening. It's truly magical when you think that the only people that could ever identify us are the victims that end up losing their lives and thereby immortalizing our efforts.

It's a certain kind of celebrity; one lived from behind a number of screens, equally factual and false. We take it because it's celebrity. We take it because of the performance.

We take it because it entertains the millions that watch.

We take it because it's ours to take.

We decided to take it. Now I'm going to ask you—

What are you going to decide?

"DON'T DO THAT! YOU SCARED THE CRAP OUT OF ME!"

YOU'RE GOING TO ASK. I know you will, so I'll get right to it. You want to know how I knew it would all work out in the end? You want to know how I knew that we'd get an offer, how I knew it would end up on the silver screen? Well, it happened with that one look, the look in the son's face, right before murdering his brother. His eyes wide, mouth dry. A gasp and a whimper. It led up to the tic, the moment of register, one feeling that overpowered him, preventing it from ending it any other way.

The look in his eyes… it was fear.

Fear is the reason for our success.

The utilization, and understanding, of what drives and directs fear is the reason why anyone performs or watches, survives and inevitably dies trying—it's the steady divvying of fear, evolving it from crime to spectacle, that made this all possible.

It's the fear that froze everyone after he showed up at the front door of the first family, asking about the power outage. It's the fear that shot up people's spines when they saw me wrap that plastic bag around the bruised and bleeding daughter.

Fear gets a person's attention. Fear is also addictive, especially when you don't know what it is. That's what I think you need to get right from the start. You're committing a crime until you turn fear upside down.

You need to turn it upside down. You need to make fear the mask that blurs your face from every single frame of footage, mask or no mask.

Fear happens to anyone that's listening, anyone that's feeling, anyone that's got something to lose. There's a change in the body as well as in a person's behavior.

* A "victim" is surrounded by fear. It's what ultimately breaks them and makes it easier on you, the "invader."

* An "invader" fears the failure and judgment of the camera. It's what ultimately tortures and tempers the performance. It's what affects the creativity of the rollout. If it turns out to be derivative, you were probably inhibited.

Fear comes from the situation at present, it'll get you turning around, looking over your shoulder, questioning what you see, and I mean really see.

It's a response that exists in a person as a sort of mechanism for survival.

Too bad then when you see that it's fear that breaks a person down.

Nobody knows how to deal with it.

What are you afraid of?

Yes.

I'm asking you.

What are you afraid of?

Is it spiders? Are you afraid of snakes?

How about death? Are you afraid to die?

Afraid of being a failure? Afraid of fucking up your performance?

Are you afraid of being alone with the camera?

Are you afraid of being rejected? Surely the cults can be unkind.

Are you afraid of heights? Are you afraid of clowns? Are you afraid of driving? Are you afraid of people?

How about speaking to others on camera or live?

Are you afraid of being attacked, becoming part of someone else's performance?

Are you afraid of being home alone?

What are you afraid of?

I'll tell you what I'm afraid of. I'm afraid of needles. Surgical needles, especially the kind that they use for spinal taps. The longer the needle, the more I feel it going in. I can feel it going in, even though it's just a needle on film caught on camera. I'm afraid of water. You have no idea how fucked up I was on that boat, when we were forcing the fourth family to drink mouthfuls of water right from the lake. When we forced them to dive for fingers, especially their own.

Fear: I was shaking the entire time.

Especially when one of the husbands struggled, which rocked the boat.

I was afraid. I had no choice but to either use it or lose it. So, I lost it. I let it sink to the bottom like the finger that kid never found.

I nearly drowned when I was young.

Fear is learned, you see. I learned to be afraid of water because of my experiences. I learned to be afraid of needles from watching so many different films and seeing how so many of us have used needles in a variety of ways, the risk never lessening.

I treat that urban legend involving infected needles being used on unsuspecting strangers as truth because the fear makes it so real.

It can be as relatable as fearing open spaces, abandoned locations (hospitals, castles, etc.), or having your heart broken. But then it gets more complicated with time. You get older, wiser (maybe), but you keep your attention trained on what you'd rather avoid. The avoidance becomes the actualization of new fears.

People develop new fears all the time.

Funny enough, they never really lose a fear. It's always there. Waiting for a signal, a nervous impulse or shock, to return.

Perhaps one day people will fear their home.

Look out into the distance. See the suburbs, the lush green.

Now look around you and see the lights beaming bright.

This is the society you live in.

The fact that you'll have done what you've wanted to do without ever being even a flicker or speck closer to being incriminated is what excites the cults that keep the cameras trained to the players, the people like you, like me, that have the same idea we all have but unlike the majority, we look up at the cameras and believe that it could happen. *Anything* could happen. Though we may be afraid, we still look.

We look up and give into the gut-wrenching feel of learning about that new limit, a new little something that sends us searching while most turn and flee from the feeling.

It keeps us worried, alive.

Fear is learned. But learning to manipulate fear gives us an edge that typically only science can give.

Do you get what I'm trying to say?

Yes?

No?

I love putting myself in the family's position. Most of the time, I'm the husband, but sometimes I'll put myself in the more vulnerable position of being a child. Never second-guess the kids though. You'll see that they're more willing to face their fears than the parents. It's one of the greatest feelings, going back and thinking about how afraid they were, what went on in their heads, how fear twisted and contorted their nerves to the point where they couldn't imagine a difference between life and death.

The moment it becomes real.

My choices changed the conditions.

I think about how the father must have felt when I asked him to tell his wife to take off her dress. I think about what the father, the sum of fear, and hate that swarmed his mind when I asked the wife to strip down while her husband and daughter watched.

It couldn't have been successful if I failed to understand how it felt for the victims—the husband, wife, sons, and daughters. I needed to know what it must feel like to be them. More so, my partner-in-performance and I both needed to be as afraid as the family. Fear surged through the victims and I saw it in their eyes. I was right there, you see? Right there, the one wearing white, the one talking and turning to the camera, part of what is now used to strike caution in the members living in the rural communities of this country. I'm not saying what we did was the first of its kind. Obviously that's not true. What I am saying is that we are our own brand of performance.

We are, with each invasion, performing something that's supposed to play on the collective fears and caution of society.

How else do you do that without tapping into your own fears?

I think about the two sons the most. Walking around with the victims, the camera caught the twinkle of in the son's eye, the gasp right before the gurgling sound of blood, hot and thick from both eye sockets, overpowered the last couple frames before cutting blank, a quick fade to white. Daylight.

The two sons fighting to the death, you just can't plan for something like that.

CHAPTER
THREE

WE'VE all got something to find and more than a little bit to lose. I'm sure we're nearly there, aren't we? We're turning left at the light, driving just under the speed limit down this street until we hit that stop sign and turn left. Another left, casual but curious, and suddenly everything narrows—the roads and the horizon, as trees, shrubs, and fences push inward, leaving us on what might be a one-way street. But it's going our way.

We're under twenty miles per hour.

We're turning right at the next juncture, if only because the other choice dead-ends, a cul-de-sac.

Where we are, it might be any neighborhood.

Where we are, it could be anything chosen, passed over, and/or made a potential point of reference. Where we are, the point of reference is a clean idea, the idea we're looking for so that we can plan it all out, plain and true.

I'm sure you're ready.

You've probably already gone around a few neighborhoods, smelled the freshly cut grass, typed in street names and house numbers into your phone, kept tallies on which houses are brightly lit at night versus those that remained completely dark, a little too good to be true.

I'm sure you've got a couple of people in mind to help you out.

You wouldn't have come to me if you weren't at least a little bit prepared.

It'll be interesting to see how well you've prepared.

Going in, you might as well be just another person walking a dog down the sidewalk, waving at other people, your would-be neighbors. You might as well be all smiles and happy. You might as well stop when someone passes by, making conversation. You might as well go on and on about your job, the really good weather—bright sunny and breezy spring day—and you might as well laugh when the dog jumps up on its hind legs and tries to lick the neighbor's face.

You might as well laugh it off, "I apologize. [Name of dog], cut that out!"

You might as well deny the neighbor's good-natured retorts.

You might as well continue walking, waving as the neighbor waves at you, a number of unneeded goodbyes when, really, you'll repeat the same thing over again tomorrow. You'll remember, but chances are the neighbor won't—and it'll be pretty much the same, repeated. You'll walk down the street like you do now, walking and turning at the corner, scanning the homes, not quite searching but more so monitoring the ebb and flow of this rural environment.

You might as well walk down this street because you'll be here tomorrow.

You'll be here every day this week.

You'll be here, maybe a new dog and a new look alternated every other day. Maybe you'll keep it the same. You'll be you, and there'll be the initial survey.

That's what this is about—getting to know the possibilities.

Within the range of possibilities, you'll choose…

And yet, you'll be the good-natured fellow met on the street, one early evening, the man with the cute dog, who maybe claimed to be a doctor or lawyer, when really, he watched, and he followed. He made sure to see where you live.

This is why we do the things we do.

We have to make a choice.

It's good to be there, if only to see how things exist before the camera switches to record.

Look at all these houses. Inside every single one is a family, a shared life made up of members that are capable of having their own too. Any of them will do. It's your pick. How do you feel? It's a great feeling, isn't it? Knowing that you have the power to choose.

Do you have a reason for choosing this neighborhood, this street, over the dozens upon dozens down the road, nearby, a couple miles away?

Fair enough, but you ought to keep in mind that there are plenty of other choices. Every home is ripe for the taking, no matter how secluded and/or secure.

Oh?

You did?

Well, that's worth a little bit of congrats and acclaim. Few go to such great lengths to research the county. But you did—you looked at the neighborhoods. You drove by and kept track of the conditions. You did all the research. You checked to see how the various neighborhoods stack up in terms of property values, income, and crime ratio. You did all that and what did you find?

Ha.

Doesn't quite add up, does it?

Yeah.

It's all about the hands-on surveillance.

It's all about looking at the houses from where you're currently standing.

It's all about just breathing in the atmosphere.

It's all about looking into the eyes of a future victim, complimenting them on a beautiful home, and then choosing theirs over so many others.

Yet, it could very well be the next door neighbor's home.

What are you looking for?

Guess we should get that out of the way.

What are you hoping to accomplish? What do you want the camera to see, what do you want to be recorded?

Perhaps it could be any one of the houses in front of us then. Yeah. You're right—it could work with pretty much any one of the families on this street.

No. You don't have to go with one now. At the same time, I should warn you though: Don't spend too much time choosing a home. They're ultimately all the same. I've heard of performances being switched midway—whole endeavors shifting to a home two blocks away, maybe more, maybe less—just because the invaders overthought the entire thing. You have to leave a little bit to chance. Remember what I said about fear? How can you be afraid if you have it all figured out?

It seems impossible having it all figured out.

So yes, you should. If you're asking...

So, you're asking. Well, yeah, you should choose.

Before ten minutes are up, you should have a home in mind.

I'll turn away, back towards your decision. Go ahead.

The suburbs are inverted. Things are not what you think they are—sure, civility is present but now crime is more curious. You pay to live in the cities. You pay to live in luxury. Many pay to be in the thick of things, the crime. Most pay because they like to be able to meet that mark. They like the feeling of being able to afford the agreed upon price.

It's as good a house as any. If you notice, it's a lot like the others: front gate, high brick wall separating it from the street. I'm sure it goes all the way around, making it impossible to get inside without either a) scaling the brick wall or b) getting through the gate. Give it a second. Take it all in. Let your senses absorb what you don't see.

The camera will go on ahead and give it the once-over.

Meanwhile, I'm going to show you how easy it is to get inside.

Watch what I do...

See?

Nothing is a blockade or barrier if it was built and/or designed by humans.

It's a nice yard. Could use a mowing. The grass is a little long. Keep note of it. It means they'll likely have someone over here soon to tend to the lawn.

Long curvy driveway leading to a three-car garage.

They leave the garage open. Also worth noting.

Two cars, a third missing. No. They have three cars. Take a look at the marks on the concrete where the rubber of the tires sat for an extensive period of time.

There's a third, maybe a fourth car.

The two that remain are parked—a convertible and an SUV. Both are moderately expensive. Both look to be in excellent shape. They keep their property clean.

The garage does not link up to the rest of the house.

That means you'll have to remember the garage as a possible location where victims might choose to hide, if given the opportunity.

It's something to consider, that's all.

Looking at the front of the house, it's got at least two stories.

But if you see how the front yard slopes down ever so slightly...

Yeah, exactly: There's a basement.

Most of these houses have not only basements but also additional crawlspace and secret entrances. But we'll get to that. At this point, you've only got the chance to survey the exterior.

You feel that?

Yes, my heart is racing too.

This never gets any easier. And that's the beauty of it.

Come on. Let's not linger around the front too long.

You never want to stick to one location. Move around. Keep your gaze wide rather than narrow. Scan the surroundings. And you should have noticed by now how they have yet to notice. The family.

You've been walking around on their property for an estimated ten minutes, but they haven't noticed us. They haven't queried the reason for our presence.

The backyard is bigger than the front. There's a treehouse in the far-right corner. Something worth considering for both future surveillance and performance factors.

Keep to a definite form. It's fine to walk around like you're here for a reason. You're really here for a reason, even though the members of the family wouldn't be quick to assume the worst. Oh yeah, sometimes they do. But if they do, it's as simple as targeting the family at a different time. There have been situations where one invader left one family for another invader. Let things cool down for a bit and it'll be fine.

They've got a deck with a little patio connected.

I can only imagine how big the interior of the house is…

I see glass sliding doors leading to the would-be basement.

See it? That's a good point-of-entry. As good as any. I'd be the type to go right in via the front door. Don't discount the blunt and bold actions.

They're usually a good way to get things going fast.

If you're looking to send a message right from the beginning, I encourage a more aggressive introduction.

But yeah. Maybe that's not quite what you have in mind.

That's good.

I respect "subtle" and "ominous."

You're looking to test the victims' senses.

You want to groom them for the big torturous payoff.

Some of the most successful performances involved a steady but subtle incline of activity, featuring a climax where the victims faced a whole set of demons.

Just because it's a home invasion it doesn't mean it needs to be about valuables—money, and the like.

The more aggressive you are, yeah, the more likely it is a smash-and-grab kind of home invasion. It feels more like a robbery.

And you don't want that.

Swing set near the far-left side of the house.

You could definitely use that.

Hmm, look at that: The roof juts up at an angle I can approximate to be designed to include a prominent attic. Those windows up there are not there for decoration. Attics are excellent for when you're hoping for a long-stay. Typically the attic has at least one compartment—an air duct or sub-entrance leading to a closet or crawlspace—wherein you can navigate during the down moments of a day when nobody is around to hear you descend. But yeah—

You're right about that.

Attics are accessible only from inside.

No, there's no real cause for worry. Those security decals can be there for illusion, but they're almost always legitimate.

Alarm systems take some time, but they almost always end up working in our favor. Ever use a duress code?

Ever heard of using an alarm system to make calls to local LAN lines?

Things get more and more creative the more you take into account the potential reverse-wiring and using of various services and systems that were installed to initially work in the house's benefit.

Besides, it's pretty common for families to keep their security low, alarm systems off, when they're home.

The most successful performances take place when the family is home.

Oh, well you look at that:

There's a gate near that patch of trees.

Hmm.

It leads to the neighbor's house.

We'll have to keep that in mind, more so than some of the other items.

Why? Think about it.

Why would there be a little gate in the brick wall infrastructure, leading to the neighbor's property? Think about it.

I want you to really think about it.

You're on the right track. It's a sign of trust.

No one installs a rickety gate to someone else's backyard if they didn't already consider the other family close friends. Perhaps this family's son or daughter likes to play in the neighbor's yard. Perhaps it's there in the event that there's danger:

They can easily flee into the neighbor's yard.

There are a number of considerations, but one that you'll need to keep clear is that it will most definitely become a part of your performance. Whether you use it or the one of the victims; the neighbor's yard, and house, will need to be factored into the performance. And just like that... you could be dealing with two homes. Two families. Two separate performances merged into one.

Getting excited. Getting good.

And finally, they've spotted us.

Now you get why I had us wear these uniforms?

They'll never suspect what you're about to do, much like they'll never suspect that their home is the one about to be invaded. It's all a blissful, boring illusion of suburbia and civility until the first stranger's footstep on hardwood floor at midnight.

Give into the fear. Use it. Just follow my lead.

Yes, hello, I'm here to service the sprinkler system. I'm not quite sure. It's all on the work-order. I can run back and get it. Yes ma'am, I tried calling but my calls weren't getting through. Not a problem. I parked 'round the corner.

Oh, that's not a problem. Everything I need I've got right here.

Yes.

By all means.

It really was a bad winter. I thought it would never end.

One warm day followed by freezing cold for three days. Hellacious. [Laughter.] Global warming. [Shrugs.]

Oh, I just need access to the control box.

Yes. It should be wherever your circuit breaker... yeah, probably in the basement.

Perfect.

And I promise to be out of your way in under a half-hour at the most.

They'll never suspect, even if they're skeptical. As long as you play along like you're as oblivious as they are to why you're there, play up innocence, and discomfort, and outright confusion, they'll be able to relate. They'll almost always think of you as just another blue-collar worker, someone that really doesn't want to be there.

Just want to get the job done and go.

But, oh watch your head there, it's a low ceiling. But look where you are now. You're inside. Wait a minute, though. Don't get carried away. You're not here to get a blueprint of the entire house. That'll come later. You're here to check on technical details—you'll need to have a look at the circuitry, the wiring, the make and model of the house's heart. The wife fed you the best possible piece of meat: talking "prime rib."

Check it out.

It's all right here.

You've got the "EKG."

You've got a look at the status of the heart.

Well, first thing you're going to do is take a couple of photos of the box, inside and out. Make sure to get all the lettering, the markings down.

Take pictures of the heater, the vents, and as much of the circuitry that runs the length of the house.

Make sure to note the width of the air ducts. You can tell just by finding the heating and/or central air system. The air pumps through those vents.

The camera's going to get everything you don't so be as meticulous as you can, even if you end up taking an extra hundred shots of nonessential material.

After you're done walk back around to the front of the house.

Knock on the front door.

You'll say something like—

That about does it. Will need your John Hancock.

A fake but believable document signed and then a little chit-chat, depending on how endearing you intend on being. Don't bother trying to peek into the house.

That'll be for another time.

You've made your choice. You've tested the waters, felt around to see what you're dealing with. The wife signs and smiles, and there are waves.

You walk back down that long driveway.

You've seen that it's a family of four, maybe five, but certainly not more.

You'll be apt to note that the husband isn't home, liking the reason for the missing third vehicle. You'll note that there may have been the sound of a younger child's voice, deeper into the house while you stood at the front door, the wife tending to the signature. But you'll also be wise to remember the swing set. Remember the treehouse. Both appeared to have been used recently—not yet neglected, as would be the case if the children had outgrown it. Enough cause to understand what you're probably dealing with. You've felt it out and I'm guessing you're liking what you see.

It was as good a choice as any.

They have attracted someone, and it might as well have been another house.

An entirely different family.

But you chose this one, and the cameras already started recording.

If you played it right, the wife will have forgotten all about you by sundown.

"THERE'S SOMEONE OUTSIDE."

THE EARLIER YOU BEGIN CASING, the stronger the setup. I should explain to you how crucial the setup is in accordance with the rest of the performance. Don't think you haven't started performing; the camera is recording. You are here, watching and being watched. The momentum will build. The performance begins with the setup. It continues with the pulloff, which is what a lot of people seem to think is the hardest part. It isn't—by then, you've got the itinerary, the various scenes and traps all figured out.

You know what you're dealing with and, what's more, they know what you're willing to do to make sure that the deal is dealt exactly the way you had planned.

After the pulloff, it's time for the spoilage. The spoilage is a grace period of sorts, an allowance for what might fail. It is the expectation of things going wrong. It's best to embrace it, knowing well that things will fall apart. You need to be ready to improvise. I've heard of invaders purposefully ruining preplanned components of the performance in order to keep themselves tense and on their toes. It can confuse the victims too, which causes disruption in what they may have already accepted to be an end, a tragedy, certain doom, of sorts. The spoilage is where it all starts to fall apart. But you see, you'll already know how much you're willing to allow, how much will spoil, before leaving.

Because you'll have to leave at some point. The aftermath acts as the sample, the first-look in what might be an outstanding project.

It all begins with the performance.

From beginning to end—the setup, the pulloff, the spoilage —that's all there is to it. But remember, you'll be watching and monitoring and making notes. You'll be auditioning for the correct partners-in-performance. I'm sure you already understand that you'll do well to have more than one by your side.

The site of the home is capable of all sorts of spoilage.

This could be a beautiful performance-in-the-making…

Or a laughable failure, right down to getting caught by authorities too soon, when, maybe, you planned on not being caught at all.

Senses open and get to work on setting both your routine and mapping theirs. Soon you'll have a map of curiosities, elements to work around for the performance to follow.

The house looks the same today, but keep in mind the differences. There will be differences and it's those little switchups and changes that'll act like leads. From your vantage point, it looks like a parked car. Perhaps it could be the parked car of a visitor. Someone somewhere on this street is having a party. Given that it's a Sunday, you have the entire afternoon to sit and watch. It's doubtful that anyone will be any wiser to your presence. Yeah, that's true: The closer it gets to nightfall, the more suspicious you'll become. But outstaying your "welcome" is worth it too. It's a good time to see how neighbors will react. How long will it take for anyone to notice? You are going to have to be aware of how curious the neighbors are. Given the private lots and the well-insulated brick walls bordering every home, I'm leaning towards there being no real problem. You could sit out here in a parked car all day. Never park in the same place twice. Go for a lot of walks. Look for more effective vantage points. From the street, you'll only see a fraction of the family's routine. I'd recommend searching for that right from the start.

Leave behind a box. Anything will do; something believable.

Yeah, something like that would work great. Look at the other houses. Notice a trend. Everyone buys online. It leaves a whole lot of empty cardboard boxes.

Leave it on their driveway.

Make it look like the wind swept it through the gate.

It's a windy afternoon.

Watch and see 1) who notices it and 2) how long it takes for that person to notice it.

The waiting is inevitable. You are going to have to be patient.

It's been an hour and a half, and no one's noticed the box. The wind has pushed it into the grass, right in plain view of any of the front windows of the house.

No movement from within the house.

It could be that no one's home.

You could tempt it—you can't even see the garage from where you are currently. This isn't going to work. You'll have to get closer. You need a better vantage point. But just think about it: No one from the street can really see into the house due to the wall enclosure. So later, when the pulloff begins, you're afforded a larger margin of error.

One of them could scream and no one will hear them from the street.

Move the car from this spot. There's really nothing else to see here. Drive down to the end of the street and towards one of the backroads leading towards the interstate.

You're going to want to park near one of the hiking trails. You'll walk it a good four miles out before making it back to the houses.

Mark your way, mapping a possible secret route for your purposes.

Forest equals concealment and privacy. It works both ways, for the watchers as much as those visible from a nearby window eating dinner.

Leave the hiking trail as early as you can, mapping your own route.

Time the entire walk.

Walk the wall, looking for faults.

In the far corner, there's a vine. See it?

Don't worry. It isn't poisonous. Test it. Give it a good tug. You can climb it.

Throw something over into the backyard.

How long did the walk take? That's not too bad. Definitely doable.

Not a sound from the other side.

That was more for potential pets.

You haven't come across an animal, but it doesn't mean that the family isn't pet-less. They might have cats. They might have a dog that lives with the family indoors.

Go ahead and climb over.

Be quick about it.

Throw your body into it. You don't want to be stuck on the top of the wall for any longer than an instant.

Okay good. Remember the rickety thin gate?

That's your destination. Move.

Keep your gaze trained to the house. Each window is equally as important and curious as the other. From the gate, look into the neighbor's yard. Keep to the shadows cast by the trees. Observe what you see. Do you see anything?

Let the camera pan across into the distance.

It's a quiet, lazy Sunday afternoon.

Perfect for your needs.

Head towards the treehouse.

This is perfect. If you lay stomach down, you can remain invisible to onlookers.

Here's vantage point #1.

Use your binoculars.

What do you see? It's dark inside but that could be due to how bright it is out here. Besides, lights wouldn't be on this early into the afternoon. Look for movement.

Safe to say that we were right. No one is home.

Go back around towards the garage.

The box is still there, where you left it.

The garage door is closed.

There's a panel on the left side of the garage.

Don't walk in a crouch. Come on. Walk like you're supposed to be here.

If anyone's going to see you, they're going to see you. The least you could do is maintain a level of confidence.

Looks like a typical security code.

Try a few of the default access codes, but don't bother with it too much.

Since you're already here, try the front door.

If someone answers, you'll look different than last time. You're wearing a suit. You're not wearing a uniform. Different identity and, really, the wife probably forgot all about you. Go ahead—

Ring the doorbell.

Give it a moment.

No matter how tense your nerves are, give it a moment.

Again—don't be obvious.

The door has paneled windows designed into its left and right sides. Can you see anything if you look?

How about a security system panel?

Okay. But nobody's home. You're free to wander around the perimeter of the house, testing possible points of entry.

Check the sliding doors. Don't pull them open. Rather, give them a slight rattle.

You don't want the alarm to go off.

Did you rattle the door?

Do it again, a little harder this time.

You'd think they'd keep it locked. This is good news. Keep in mind of motion detectors and other additive forms of security.

It's up to you. You want to go in?

Might as well keep going. You're already here.

Here goes nothing...

The family, it turns out, has a typical security system, one that remains off until—you can assume—late night.

It's not on right now. But in each room, you will want to note all motion detectors, unlock all windows that are free from any security devices. Be meticulous about it. This is about preplanning. Before you can start with performance-building scenes, you need to know what it's like inside the house. The basement, we've already discovered, is used as a neglected playroom and storage space. There's a tiny bar with dusty glasses and wine/liquor that goes untouched. Two of the four rooms in the basement are full of boxes. The biggest room has a billiards table, two arcade cabinets, one pinball machine, and a large and accommodating television and wrap around leather couch. The television, you'll notice, is unplugged. Nobody uses the basement.

This is vantage point #2.

You've tracked the security system and its various installations. You've noted the first floor and how it remains open in a way where both voices and footsteps echo on hardwood, high-ceilinged accommodations. The kitchen is the most-used room in the entire house. See how the windows from the stove, and sink, look out towards the swingset, the backyard, whereas, the treehouse, higher up on one of the largest trees in the yard, is just out of focus, pushed towards the right.

Vantage point #1 will be of great use in the week(s) ahead.

Note the matching bowls set near the cabinets.

As expected, the family has a dog.

This is curious. Let's hope you don't have to contend with multiple pets. Long before there were security systems, dogs were used to ruin a performance.

But remember: We don't have to let it ruin what's being recorded.

You can use it to your advantage. It's why we are here.

Don't start moving things around. Not yet.

Wait until tomorrow morning.

Begin mapping the routines of each family member. You can learn so much by the look and smell of a person's bedroom. Few ever really take advantage of kid's bedrooms. Keep that in mind. Craft secret. Hint, hint. Vantage point #3—clearly a young daughter's room. It might be of some use, especially since the master's bedroom is on the other side of the second floor. A guest bedroom is across from the daughter's room.

This next room…

Expensive stereo system in the far corner.

Laptop on the bed, left open.

Clothes strewn about, many of them dress shirts, studded belts, and jeans.

You find some porn magazines shoved underneath the bed.

This is a prototypical teenage male's bedroom.

See what I mean about things almost always telling a story all on their own? You'd be surprised how stereotypical people's rooms become, right on down to how they drape their walls in posters and other items of expression. The teenage male thought to put up band posters, a few basketball players caught mid dunk. Spot the pinup calendar. Guitar with a broken string. It's a story we've all heard, and maybe lived.

The master bedroom has two walk-in closets.

Husband owns a plethora of suits, many of them expensive. Note the safe in the back. If you decide to play up a would-be robbery, there's something to keep in mind. I wouldn't recommend it though, because then you get them talking about money, and that's some of the worst dialog a performance can have.

Keep it confusing for them, like there really is no reason for the invasion, and the performance will be that much better.

Trust me.

The wife's got so much stuff she has a second room full of clothes. There's no bed in this one, and it appears as though the room has multiple purposes. The slanted desk complete with a few blueprints is a clear giveaway.

Don't bother looking for one of these homes. You're going to have to memorize every single corner of it either way.

Better to do it via hands-on survey.

It appears as though the husband might be an architect.

Their backstories play out predictably no matter how much you know beforehand. Best to keep to concrete details:

Age.

Gender.

Daily routine.

And maybe fears, if only for when you start up with the tempting, the teasing, which you'll soon have to do in order to test their resilience.

Go back to vantage point #3. The daughter's room.

Check the window. It doesn't have a motion sensor.

Keep that window unlocked.

Check the closet. Now look at that…

Talk about lucky.

It's a crawlspace.

Might as well give it a glance. It's big enough to hide in, but that's not why you should note just how lucky you are. The vent connected to it isn't big enough for you, but it might be the perfect means of transporting materials between floors.

I'm excited for you.

Few get a chance to survey and case the target from this close.

You'll be able to hear the daughter sleeping.

It's truly a rare occurrence.

It's often easier to squat in the house for days, moving things around, setting an atmosphere of oddity, than leaving and returning. You need to factor in how every single visit increases the odds of being discovered two-fold.

Some of the most successful performances were marathons of surveillance and voyeurism in and of themselves. Given the sensitivity of your situation, how you may have already been seen by a nosy neighbor or left some kind of trace that might grab the attention of a member of the family, you'll want to stick around.

I know that you know exactly what I'm implying.

You had to have understood that you would have to do this at the onset, at least for a few days. It's why you have those rations; it's protein. The liquid tastes horrible, but this is for the sake of the performance.

You're already here.

Think about having to leave the crawlspace, going back down the stairs, into the basement, out into the yard where you might be spotted by a neighbor that just happened to be home and felt like enjoying the sunny day. Back over the brick wall, into the woods, out into the nothingness of that four-mile walk: This could be you.

But if you're smart, you'll do what I'd do given your situation.

You've got a hell of an opportunity here.

You'll be able to learn all about the family in half the time.

Everything you don't see, the camera will record. You'll settle in for the night. Don't bother making a sound. Rest in the crawlspace. Ignore any and all discomfort.

Recall the reason for doing this at all.

You have to be ready to move and react. You'll want to be able to watch as the family goes about their day.

It's about to get even more curious.

If you ask me, the key to any great home invasion is that the act must be senseless. Surely no act is senseless but, in this case, it must at least appear to be. No financial motive. No reason for revenge. It is pure fun, by chance; make it appear as though it could have been anyone. Make it clear that it can and will happen to anyone.

That's why I think it's good to start with this.

You'll want to make it something bold, something that gets them scared right from the start. But, you see, you can't have them calling 911 at the beginning. Think in layers. Remember, the layering of subtlety and suspicion?

You're testing the waters, checking to see their resilience. You aren't here just to mess with them. That's a perk, for sure; but it's a small part of the performance.

You want to shatter a window or write something heinous on one of the bathroom mirrors. You want to provoke them so fully, and I get it—I was the same way. We're all anxious to get it going quickly. But you've got so much more to do. Don't forget that you still need to identify routines and roles.

You still need to plan out the baseline, how those ideas of yours will be able to connect scene-to-scene and, in the grand scheme of things, make complete sense.

For the act itself is senseless, but the performance:

The camera was made for this kind of drama.

A drama so real, it sends shivers down the spines of everyone that watches, and that includes the ones that have seen it all. If you can get the cults clamoring for analysis, you'll have figured this all out. You'll have become a success, with or without the instant draw of a studio executive's interest.

So then wait until early morning to begin meeting the members of the family.

You can be there just before they wake up.

You can keep count and build the unsettling atmosphere.

The slow and steady rise: The great ones take their time.

Stick to my choice. Remember that you came to me, asking for my aid.

When the family returns, gate opening and the SUV pulling into the driveway, they'll see that the garage door is open. The husband, the one driving, will instinctively tap the button to open the garage door. Due to it having already been, it'll begin the process of shuttering its paneled doors.

The wife will blame the husband, "You forgot to close the garage door?"

Yet it's with this simple and assumed act of disregard that you've made your first declaration. This ultimately meaningless gesture is your introduction, your greeting. Your way of saying hello. How fitting, then, when they move past it in moments, moving on with the remainder of their night. Like nothing is going to happen. Like nothing is going to change. It's been a busy day, but you're where you are, and your vehicle is parked where nobody will find it. At least not before you return and fetch it for more supplies.

How fitting that you'll be able to walk the halls like you live there, the motion sensors and illusion of security, much like silence, kept undisturbed as you are a person, getting to know the layout of the house, the feeling of having the family there with you, living in a blissful state that they'll never really appreciate, not until the pulloff begins.

The daughter saw the box. She picked it up and brought it inside the house. The wife asked her, "Where did you get that?"

Daughter didn't reply. "What did I tell you about touching icky things?" The wife broke down the box and tossed it in the recycling bin in the laundry room.

You have three vantage points—
#1, the treehouse.
#2, the basement.
#3, the daughter's room.

CHAPTER
FIVE

THE HALLWAY IS empty during these pre-dawn moments, when the windows are merely windows, nothing more to cause alarm. Got to love these moments. You shouldn't be so quick to get around the house. You're still casing but I think it's worth a few extra breaths and nervous heartbeats to enjoy the way it feels to be in the privacy of someone else's home. Just... stand there, at the foot of their bed. Just stand there, watching the husband toss and turn in his sleep. Listen to the wife talk in her sleep. Whisper a reply—

"I look forward to meeting you."

Walk the hall. Stop at the top of the stairs.

Breathe in. Breathe out.

Feels great huh?

This could almost be your home, imagining that you're simply up later than the rest of the family, or awake earlier than most. Note the locked door, the teenage son valuing his privacy. I wouldn't worry about it; it's an easy lock. A quick turn and tumble with a tool and you'll be looking down at the one most likely to cause problems.

But we'll get to that later.

Back in the daughter's room, be careful: you shut the door a little too hard. The sound almost woke her up. She's a light sleeper. But it was obvious when you first exited the closet. It's almost dawn, so you take a quick look and see that the daughter may have seen you. She'll look and see a shadow and maybe, to her, you're a monster.

However, the daughter is a little too old to believe in monsters.

Be careful with this one. There's no telling what she's already seen.

See what I mean now? Keeping a tally will reveal the routines of each member of the family. Each member will tell you their entire story based around the things they do every day, without fail. It's because they have to do these things, and want to fit in the other activities, that establish who they are.

And you are here to figure out exactly who they are.

There can only be one set of strangers, and they are the invaders watching from windows, from close by, a shorter distance than any victim would ever expect.

The important stuff goes right onto the page. After seeing it happen a few times, you won't even second-guess their actions. You'll know the ins and outs of their day.

The rest of it, we'll get to that later. I know I say that a lot but it's true. It's all baby steps until the performance reaches step two, the pulloff.

The family has a pet dog, a German Shepard. Its crate is in the kitchen. It sleeps there at night and doesn't usually bark unless there's an intruder. Early observation casts the dog in neglect. The wife pours food in the dog's bowl and refills the water dish whenever it's empty. Other than that, the dog walks the house, follows around the sunlight cast on the hardwood floors, snoozing and sunbathing, until it needs to go outside. The wife takes care of that too. If not, perhaps it's the daughter. The dog's routine is more or less the same. It is not uncommon for the dog to toss a ball around by itself, perhaps hoping one of the members will hear and join in. That doesn't happen though. You might as well.

Kind of feel sorry for the dog, right?

Go ahead. Say hello to the dog.

By 7AM, the son has left for school. By 8AM, both husband

and wife leave for different purposes. The husband is off to work. That's the last we'll see of the guy until late into the night. The husband is never home any earlier than 9PM.

The wife brings along the daughter and returns alone, presumably having dropped off the daughter at school. The wife remains, more or less remaining, on the bottom floor of the house, near the kitchen, watching television and sticking to the laptop set up on the kitchen counter. She won't leave until 2:45PM. She's never late. It's the only item on her to-do list. Rest of the day, she's wafting in a haze of sorts. Really seems strange, I know, but then again, I think you're right: The wife isn't happy. The wife is clearly affected by what is already lining up to be a textbook case of home and abroad in shambles. The family, for being in such a financially capable situation, seems to run on the fumes of some near and dire collapse.

Didn't you see how the son ignored his parents?

Didn't you see how the wife and husband failed to look at each other in the eye, barely even giving each other a kiss, and probably wouldn't have if it weren't already built up via years of routine?

And the house itself remains in a state of half-disuse.

It is worth considering the fact that there might be a maid service at some point.

No, I wouldn't be worried. You have time.

It doesn't appear as though it'll happen over the next day or so.

The wife fails to eat anything all day.

It isn't until after she returns home with the daughter—who, on all accounts, seems to be the lone member in the brightest mood—that she feasts on snacks. Look at all those cookies and chips and other junk food. The wife is good at playing happy mother. She seems to have completely transformed since returning with the daughter. The afternoon at home consists of the wife being a happy, cheery mother, helping the daughter with her homework, spoiling the daughter by letting most of the day waste away via watching television, occasionally playing in the backyard, the swing-set, never near vantage point #1—the treehouse. Once, only once, and typically only in the late afternoon, around the time the son returns home from school, will there be another child, about the same age as the daughter, walking through the rickety fence, from the other side of the brick wall. The wife does her best to seem interested in the neighbor's conversation, but you can tell, even from where you are, the view from the daughter's bedroom window, that the wife is going through the same motions.

The son shows up around 4:30-5PM. He doesn't announce his arrival and the wife appears to have given up asking. The daughter waves hello. The son glances but doesn't wave back and storms up the stairs, locks his door and will not show his face until around 8PM when dinner is served.

The wife doesn't cook. She has an extensive binder of menus for places that deliver. The wife has a delivery service on speed dial. The wife asks the daughter. The same exchange happens every night:

"What you in the mood for?"

"Dunno. What does dad want?"

It's how the wife sort of hesitates, almost losing the façade; proves that it isn't the first, and certainly won't be the last time this happens.

Every night it has been the same.

The wife has her line queued, "You know daddy has a lot of work to do."

Seems rehearsed, doesn't it? From where you are, vantage point #2, the basement, you can hear it all. Up a couple more steps and you can see that it's the wife and the daughter at the kitchen table. No one else. The son doesn't show until he's been texted by the wife. The son sits down and eats quickly. There's no dinner conversation. The food cartons go right in the trash and there's really nothing for the wife to clean up.

The daughter lingers around after dinner, but only because of the television downstairs. By now the wife is back to her laptop. She tunes out most of what the daughter does. The daughter leaves before the husband returns home. One night it was around 9PM. Another night it was closer to 10. Some nights, we can imagine him not returning home at all.

The wife stays up, but it looks like it could be that she can't sleep without pills.

The daughter calls from the upstairs hallway, "Mommy?"

It's bedtime. It's 10:10PM.

The wife goes upstairs. I know it's tough to outline this particular part of the evening because you've only got muffled audio, whatever you hear from the cracks of the crawlspace. It's fine. This is all about feeling out the interior spaces of the performance. This is about understanding the innermost spaces of privacy.

The husband returns at 11:30PM. He doesn't offer an excuse to the wife because by then the wife has gone to bed. The next day is only a slight variation of this.

You've probably got enough to go on but see we're all in waiting until someone notices.

It's a good sign, for you, when they finally notice the dog missing.

It took them more than a day.

And it was the daughter that noticed on the off chance that she dropped cereal to the floor and some of it got in the water dish. Leave bits of cereal in water all day and you'll see that they will begin to puff up and turn soggy, nearly liquid too.

The daughter notices how the water has grown cloudy.

Fibers from the cereal have formed a ring around the water line.

The wife, with daughter in tow, walks around the house, calling out the dog's name. Wait a minute—maintain your distance.

Stay a couple steps behind. Don't get too close. I know you're getting to a point where it's becoming predictable. The camera's got it tied down too. Still, you don't want them to notice you in the mid-day sunlight. This is methodical. This is methodical research. Think of it as such. You're going to have to test the waters. Can't do that if you get caught this early in.

It's a systematic search for the dog, the one they won't find.

It's the highlight of the night.

Daughter tells the son, who disinterestedly blames the wife, "Maybe mom let it out and it ran away."

The wife's fault, it's always the wife's fault.

It can't be the other parent if he's never around. The son is back in his room.

You've already been in there, right? Did you gather the necessary information?

Screen names, IP address, account numbers, email addresses?

Excellent. No, you won't need direct access to any accounts. Who needs to hack into anything if you're already on their friend's list?

At bedtime, the daughter asks the wife, "Where do you think she went?"

The wife offers a bunch of possibilities but neither wife nor daughter can be very confident of what are essentially lies.

The dog has run away, and the daughter asks about making fliers to put around the neighborhood. The wife lies and says, "Sure sweetie." But even we know it's illegal to do that in this neighborhood. The dog remains missing until needed to play out its role in the performance.

From vantage point #1, the treehouse, you can see how the husband makes a conscious effort to avoid the wife. Right before leaving a room, the husband listens for the wife.

He sneaks around.

When he's near her, he goes cold.

I'm sure you can't hear anything. You don't know how to read lips, do you?

Didn't think so.

Husband does his best not to leave a trace.

But that isn't the wife on the phone as he pulls out of the driveway. It couldn't be the wife that's able to bring that grin on the husband's face. It couldn't be the wife that says beautiful, muted nothings, getting the grin to form into a laugh as he disappears.

That couldn't be the wife because she's watching from her bedroom window.

I'm sure you can see her from where you're standing.

If the wife looked down, she could have spotted you there, framed by a first-floor window, waving back at her.

The wife doesn't pick up the daughter today, later to be discovered that the daughter had attended a sleepover, another kid's birthday party, which means the wife watches television, cowering under a blanket for the remainder of the evening. The son returns home and heads upstairs.

The wife switches channels.

The wife forgets to eat.

The son leaves at around 8PM.

He won't return until 2AM.

The husband doesn't return, not after the would-be argument that transpired, and he won't return until the following evening.

The wife falls asleep around 10PM.

She wakes up when you turn off the television. It's the first time she's stood up from the couch since that afternoon. Didn't notice the difference.

Use the shadows, the darkness of the late night, empty house, to watch from the other room as the wife wanders into the bathroom, raids the fridge for random stuff to eat, and returns to the couch.

It's only now that she notices that you've switched off the power.

Walk right up to the couch. Stand there, observing as she falls back asleep.

It's unfortunate. The camera captures the quickest, most honest take.

Seeing this, it makes me wonder if there are a lot of families living this way—so distant and broken apart, hiding under the illusion of something idyllic.

The cults love seeing the dream, picket white fence and beautiful homes, upturned and cut into surgical slices, for viewing. It's a look into a private space that, if the wife isn't a perfect example, I don't know what is, may very well be far worse that the performance to follow. The wife sleeps only because she has no reason to be awake.

She won't wake up again until morning.

I think it's a great idea, yeah. Definitely go through with it. It's not like the husband really wears all those suits. Put them in the garage. Box them up and place the box where the convertible usually is. Nothing wrong with a little creativity.

The camera gets the entire fight because you clearly couldn't have been there, not if you had been in the basement for most of the evening, triple-checking the heart of the house before leaving tonight. Wife in the master's bedroom. The husband in the office. It is a tense night for both of them. In the hallway, you can hear the wife in tears.

In the office, you brush a finger across the back of the husband's neck.

I still find that so daring. You're a natural you know that?

Why do you need me here?

I mean really?

This is an argument you and I could certainly have—there's plenty of time for that—but between the distant measures data that can be used for the performance and the little things we couldn't ever plan, those spells of creativity, I know that you've got potential. You've only just begun but already you figured out how to bond with the family. You have walked right up to them and they haven't noticed.

Yeah, okay, that's a stupid thing to say.

However, you've essentially done just that, and we now have it on camera. We have it all recorded, splayed like how I imagine you'll want their dead bodies to be splayed at the very end. I'm going to ask you some questions—

Does the wife know now about the husband's affair?

Thought so.

What's going to happen next?

And she's just going to stick around?

The wife's not leaving him?

I tell you, it's feels like people don't know how to deal with a problem.

The daughter, their son—they stay together because of their kids, perhaps; but it doesn't make much of a difference when the money's going to be halved.

I could ask you if they got a prenuptial, and you'd probably have already checked into that. See what I mean?

You're a natural.

I'm only here because a member of the cult ought to be included.

But then again, we're all members, in some way, shape, and form.

The camera captures a wonderful shot that sends goose bumps into those that will watch later. It's a shot of a flashlight in the dark. It's the shot of you, walking the house, shining the light one last time across surfaces, in the eyes of the sleeping family members.

The wife doesn't so much as budge.

The father turns on his side, away from the light.

The son's eyelids twitch. The son almost wakes up.

The daughter wakes up.

What are you going to say? I think you can come up with something, anything I might. Are you sure? Well, okay. If you insist on needing it. Yeah, just follow my lead.

Hello.

"Hi..."

Don't mind me.

She's rubbing her eyes. Can't keep them open, much less focus on your face.

Do it.

Shine the flashlight in her face. The daughter won't be able to see past the light. She won't be able to see your face.

"Are you Daddy's friend?"

Am I? Did your daddy say I was his friend?

"Mommy and Daddy were fighting about Daddy's friend."

Mommies and Daddies fight sometimes.

Mommy and Daddy still love each other.

Is something the matter, sweetie?

"Are you looking for her?"

Who?

"My dog. She went missing and..."

She's fading. Just keep talking.

Say—I am. I'm looking around. I got my trusty flashlight and everything.

"Are you going to find her?"

I won't stop until I do.

"She ran away... and she..."

Shh—sleep now.

She's not going to remember. But just in case, whisper the words—

I'm a friend of the family.

I'll find her.

Kiss her on her forehead, mimicking what her mother or father would do, if she had woken up from a nightmare and required their aid and assurance.

But I wouldn't think you're too worried about any of it, are you?

Yeah, didn't think so. When all is said and done, the wife and husband won't think much of the daughter's claims. If she remembered, it'll be something thought of by anyone that might hear as a fabrication, some little dream or a fantasy built around a young imagination. You can shine that flashlight all over the entire house and no one's going to bother. The house, so late at night, is yours.

You do this because you want to do this.

Brilliant. It's brilliant, and I mean what I say. You only needed to set up the basics and already you've become a bonafide observer and provocateur.

It's impressive. I want you to know that you're a natural. It's like you're an open book and everything you do is a line that comes to life in the reader's mind.

Moreover, I want you to believe it.

Embrace it.

You can't help but keep going, like a reader that can't help but turn the pages, craving the next scene.

We've seen a lot.

I think you've seen enough.

Can you picture the house, the family members' faces, when you close your eyes? Can you conjure up a basic profile? Can you more or less predict what they'd be doing at any given point in the day/night?

Then good.

You're ready.

You've got everything you need. It's a walk through the forest by moonlight, but no worries, the camera's got night vision. You'll be fine.

I know the dog's heavy. Who would have thought a dog's body would feel like carrying a boulder? Keep things in perspective. I'm telling you:

You'll be fine.

I'll talk you through it. Next time you enter their property, you won't be alone. Never mind what's behind the camera, you'll have an entire crew—partners-in-performance—who will help carry the bodies, carry the case, and canvas the house in order to make this performance successful.

The voice in your ear, it's just the cults clamoring about, looking to understand, quick to speak the word "disturbing," only to inevitably settle on fascination.

It's all so fascinating.

Can't you hear me?

"DID YOU HEAR THAT?"

THERE ARE names on birth certificates and names spoken when addressed, names on newspaper bylines and names tattooed on human skin, but there'll be no names mentioned, no names cast across this performance. The moment an invader is named, it's the same as with a victim, like any member of the family you've cased extensively: The performance suffers, and the details drown out curiosity. It clouds the image on camera. It makes everything seem like just another act of violence when violence is the least important part of your performance.

There will be no names assigned.

There will be no names on file.

It doesn't have to be this way.

It's merely better this way. The cults get at it and it becomes an ongoing scenario, played up and down, in mind and matter, for posterity's sake and, you hope, prosperity's sake. The authorities fill in the details later. You create the puzzle. The performance mystifies but the authorities secretly love it. They are members of the cults, much like everyone else that may be looking, watching, seeking out more than just a headline or blurb about the performance.

Keep the definitions clear, the concepts in frame, so you can tell the difference between invader and victim, curiosity from fear.

And that, my friend, will make for the most beautiful experience.

The family consists of four members (five if you want to count the dog)—the husband, who is also a father, the wife, who is also a mother, the daughter, who has the possibility of surprising you every step of the way, and the son, who is every bit a teenager as any other, as best evidenced in the angst and disregard towards would-be dangers.

The family plays the role of victims.

In order—

Victim #1—husband.

Victim #2—wife.

Victim #3—daughter.

Victim #4—son.

Alternate roles are numerous. But, yeah, you're right, not to worry. They remain, as they are, a family, a father, a mother, a child, and a child. Wouldn't dare change the roles they've been wearing as alternates, but you should keep in mind what those alternate roles are. What do I mean? Well, just think—how else can they play a victim if they're only two-dimensional? As a husband, he's never around and certainly neglectful. He has grown apart with both family and wife. But how is he as a father—no, there's a difference. How does he view his children? How do the children view him? It's just an example, that's all. You'll have to know how they're played so that the camera captures the right angle, the right side of their role.

No problem. I figured I'd save you the trouble of having to audition hundreds of eager members. The cults aren't what they used to be—it's a mess of all sorts of personalities, many of them fake. Yeah. It happens whenever the scene becomes more of a, well, scene. Starts small like anything else but if there's any success, and it's encouraging to have seen so many successful performances yield to the silver screen, to popular culture, more eyes will turn to the dark outlines of danger.

Civility is for the commercial taglines. Keep creativity within the cult.

I want you to know that I did it for the craft.

For the sake of the craft, I offer you these, perfect partners-in-performance.

Thanks, but no thanks, really. They're just good for the part, good for your needs.

Well, I'm flattered, but if you insist, thank me by following through. We've all got to start somewhere. Might as well help someone start closer to the camera, help them get the better shots, better angles, you know?

It couldn't be anything else than that.

My motivations are selfless save for the sole exception:

I want to be entertained like anybody else. So what if it takes all this to get us there? We're captivated by the craft; we're too smart to believe in the gates, fences, the silence of so-called rural privacies.

If there's an address, there's a possibility.

You see, this one's for you.

The performance has its crew, and you are its lead. Surprised?

It's okay.

I'm just joking around.

You are invader #1.

In addition to your role, you have two other partners. They're good people.

Yeah—oh you did? Good to hear. It helps to have bonded over a night of alcohol and good conversation. My partner-in-performance kept everything confidential. It was business through and through. I refuse to say it wasn't mutual, given the nature of our performance; if we really had any knowledge of each other's private lives, we might have ended up using them in our improvisational skits. At one point, I chastised him, mockingly, of course, about having sexual relations with his mother.

Yeah, it was purely for effect.

So, there's two—

Invader #2 and invader #3.

I'm impressed—this is thinking outside of the box. Where did you meet this person? Oh, I see. And you don't have a problem with being blood relatives?

It's good to have someone in the family that shares the same hobby.

He will be given the role of "voice," one that walks the line between victim and invader, typically donning the role of insider. The "voice" will befriend a victim to help facilitate certain scenes of the performance. The "voice" doesn't usually pose for the camera, choosing to be more out-of-focus and suspicious—at least to those watching from behind the camera. To the family, your relative will be someone suddenly compassionate and dear, ultimately to suffer from one of their mistakes.

Oh, I'm just talking. I'm sure you've got it figured out.

No. You don't have to tell me.

I want to be surprised. It has become so difficult to be surprised.

Believe me, it's important. Never forget the importance of entertainment.

For multi-stage performances, it's better to compartmentalize the duties.

I suggested a backup crew, especially if you intend on creating a two-fold stage. You cannot maintain both stages, much less all the scenes, big and small, that will play out as the performance bleeds on through the night. Okay, you can—yet I still think it's better to acquire an additional crew.

Oh, I think two more partners will do. Trust me.

Give them a little bit of autonomy. You will have to allow for it.

Their primary duty will be to spoil.

Invader #4 and invader #5—they remain a secret to the camera until it's their cue.

Typically, there are subordinate victims—maids, butlers, babysitters—but you have little to worry about here. The house remains pristine and routinely predictable.

If there's a babysitter, she'll be the one of the performance's first witnesses.

Perhaps she'll be the one that calls in the authorities.

It's worth keeping an eye on the neighbors.

Keep them in mind for the spoilage portion of the performance.

Victim #1 as husband is, on all accounts, disinterested in his significant other. He maintains a passive-aggressive demeanor, favoring distance via long hours at work.

There is a mistress, an affair, well in the works, as means of relief as well as possible countermeasure to his significant other's misgivings.

Tension remains high and, as husband, the role has devolved to maintaining the institutions of marriage and family. Little else can be drawn from the role.

As husband, victim #1 is subpar at best.

Victim #1's sole alternative—father. As father, one child is favored over the other. He nurtures the very basic minimums needed to remain relevant in the daughter's life. Based on the casing, were you able to find out any exact details?

That's unfortunate.

It's not important. We can assume that as father, he buys the daughter what is desired and takes up the opportunity to spoil the daughter at every juncture.

As father, his relationship with the son ranks in lowest, much lower than the marital turmoil. That's quite low—what do you base this on?

I see. Then as a father, he fails to exist in the son's daily routine. They cross paths once, in the morning, when neither is willing to say much more than "good morning."

Victim #1 retains his distance from the situation of the house that he could mistake another residence as his own and so there is no issue of him discovering the camera.

Victim #2 as a wife is overcome with clinical depression. She has seen someone.

Are you certain? What's the label on the bottle say?

Hmm, interesting—she has been suffering for years. It would account for her inactivity, and the precision with which she performs her role as wife, making the right appearances— seemingly cheery small chat with the neighbor, a "fun" afternoon with the daughter—while retaining the actuality of her emotions a secret.

As a wife, she has been performing the role with little to no feeling for an extended duration, much longer, perhaps, than most.

Victim #2's sole alternative—mother. As mother, she has only the one child to interact with, given that her other child, who has long since outgrown his mother's love, negates any efforts as false, fake, fabricated. The reason for this could be due to the son's ability to see through the charade, her performance.

As mother, she tends to the daughter as much as she can muster. By all accounts, it's well enough that the daughter fails to notice a difference. She drops off and picks up the daughter. She drives the daughter to extracurricular activities. She spends the majority of her time on the computer, a laptop in the kitchen. Groceries, supplies and all other needs are delivered—there's no telling that she ventures any farther out than the two destinations—school   and   home—encompassing   her   daily routine.

Despite victim #2 spending the most time in the house, she is least likely to be aware of the camera.

Victim #3 as a daughter retains a certain naivety to the reality that has already begun to surround her on all sides. She has no routine to maintain for her life is one of few responsibilities and only a handful of expectations. As daughter, she has yet to outgrow her mother; as well, she has yet to see through her father's shoddy attempts at maintaining relevance in his daughter's life. Were you able to gather any details about her friend(s) identities? It's not a problem but figured it would be worth outlining too.

Don't worry about it. If there is going to be any intrusion, it would have to first pass through the planning stages, one that involves both victim #2 and a coinciding parent, discussing play dates and other child outings.

Victim #3's sole alternative—a child, because she is still very much a child. She will be less likely to look away; she will be more likely to observe the subtle changes that incur around the house. Though, as a child, she will be able to scare easier than the rest of the family, she may very well discover the sources far sooner than the others merely because she will be too curious, too impressionistic to look away.

Victim #3 is most likely to notice the camera; in fact, she might have seen it the one night, while cast in flashlight. It's definitely worth noting.

It might become something, yes.

But for now, it is data, liner notes, stuff that the partners-in-performance should know about. I wouldn't dare say that we aren't already well aware of the possibilities with this one.

Victim #4 as a son is predictably a teenager, dealing with the angst-ridden issues and the apathy that trails by with every single action. As a teenager, he could be doing alright. There isn't a whole lot to be garnered from the casing, save for all the information gathered online. But we'll get to that. What is known, for sure, is that, as a son, he has a room upstairs to call his own. He takes advantage of both room and board. Meals are his, when he feels like eating. Most of the time, a vehicle is missing in the garage and so is he.

Victim #4's sole alternative—a child, is less appropriate given that neither parent views him as a child. He is likely to become more akin to the father—conveniently busied with career and external relationships/roles outside of the house, outside of the family.

Given the distance, and disregard, victim #3 wouldn't be aware of the camera until long after the performance, around the time records leak and the cults begin ripping it apart via analysis.

What mask are you wearing?

Actually, I think it's best to have one lead and number of alternatives.

Oh right—I assumed you already understood. I mean it can be that. It can be exactly what you want it to be. It's called a "mask," but it's not to be confused with the fact that many choose to wear a physical mask. It could be something as simple as a mindset—that can be your mask, as "invader"—but the term remains the same because the act of donning is identical.

You wear roles to better fit the performance. You wear roles to fit the demands of the camera. You wear roles so that you remain anonymous, a character well-casted for the role. You wear a mask to conceal and to best capture the scene at play.

You'll need plenty, I gather.

You'll need to be able to look right in the camera and fail to notice it looking back at you. So, to do that, in my case, I wore white gloves, casual yet fashionable dress, not unlike what someone would be caught wearing in a neighborhood like the one we targeted, and I became the role. It was the gloves, for me. That was the item in the entire outfit that helped me create that masking of identity. At one point, my partner-in-crime donned another mask, one of half-victim, when I started verbally attacking him for the sake of the performance. However, I never had an alternative. You'll have to think about whether or not you'll need many for you and the other invaders.

Think about it. Oh, and you don't have to wear gloves if you choose to factor in this as your one and only performance.

You can choose to end it that way.

Prison sentences are poetic in a sense.

Again, just saying.

As invader #1, you can wear a ski mask or a ghoul mask or a fox mask or a pig mask or a tiger mask or a smiley mask or a cupid mask or a demon mask or a phantom mask or a grinning mask or a Reagan mask or a skull mask or a rabbit mask or a hockey mask or a ghostface mask or a dead celebrity mask or a dollface mask or a buccal mask or a luchador mask or a gas mask or a balaclava or a fencing mask or a welding mask or a ritualistic hood or a goblin mask or a faceless mask or a Venetian mask or a biker helmet or a clown mask or a zipper mask or a stocking or a surgical mask or a Noh mask or a death mask or a mask that is of your own design.

You have only one mandatory mask, and it's your role as lead, your role as the one that pulls the trigger, stabs first, without hesitation, and beyond anything to do with violence, you wear the mask of the one that walks in first and leaves last; you are the one that speaks to the victims, makes commands and chooses to quicken or slow the momentum of the scene as it happens. As lead, you are not unlike a director, if a performance such as this could be directed.

That is your mask. That is your imperative.

Other than that, choose to look how you'd like.

As invader #2, he can wear a mask of his choice or that of his or your own design.

He has only one mandatory mask, and it is to maintain the performance, following suit with the actions needed in and around each scene. If you aren't there to act, he must be there to take over. If you need help, he must be there. Not in a minute. Not two moves later. Now. I can't stress it enough.

There is no alternative:

Partners-in-performance must move like one whole unit, one body, not a group of parts but one seamless entity, walking in step. Use the "dance" analogy if you like.

I feel like you understand.

That is his mask. That is his imperative.

Invader #2 follows the lead of invader #1. It is as simple and important as that.

As invader #3, he can wear a mask of his choice or that of his or your own design.

He has only one mandatory mask, and it is to maintain the performance, following suit with the actions needed in and around each scene. If your number #2 isn't there to act, he must be there to fill in. If you or #2 needs help, he must be there. And then there's the necessitation of joint actions, because it won't be enough to lure a victim all by yourself. Sometimes it will require you, a partner, maybe both. There will be scenes where the entire crew is in action.

There is no alternative:

Partners-in-performance must move like one whole unit, one body, not a group of parts but one seamless entity, walking in step. Use the "dance" analogy if you like.

Yeah, I repeated myself. It's brutally important.

That is his mask. That is his imperative.

Invader #3 trails by invader #2 but follows your lead.

As voice, he wears no physical mask; rather, his facial features are accentuated with prioritized gestures and perhaps cosmetically altering makeup, used sparingly.

The voice must match the likeness of the victim.

The voice must be ready to don a number of alternatives. And yes, that includes your role, the roles of your partners, including the backup crew.

The voice must be a friend, a neighbor, a postal employee/deliveryman, a phone call when needed. He must be the one the cults least suspect. The voice is comprised of nothing but alternatives. He'll be a chameleon, the one set to disrupt, deny, and dig up details based on the conditions of the performance.

The voice's mask is to make it seem like he's harmless, believable.

If he's really good, he'll break the family's heart. You know, when it comes time.

You did tell your relative how his part will end, right?

As invaders #4 and #5 wear the mask of contradiction. They mask secrets. They are secrets. I don't want to go too much into their roles, but a little bit like how voice will act, the backup crew is like a shadow. Your crew's shadow. If you hear footsteps from behind, odds are it's them, following. They wear the mask of spoiling your performance.

As long as you are able to maintain his and her roles, moving in unison especially when it looks, to the victims, to the camera, like you both are moving against each other, fighting for the same scenes, you will be fine.

I'm excited just thinking about how #5 will use victim #4.

I'm excited about what you told me #4's going to do.

Really? That's great. It will lessen the burden of managing some of the more subtle scenes. I'm excited. This is going to be great.

Oh, have you forgotten about the dog?

Good, because it will come in handy.

Everyone's a victim unless you're wearing the right "mask." Think more about the role, the action, and response. That's what I'm trying to say. It's important. One of the most important details. Besides, the camera blurs out everyone's faces.

I told you that, remember?

CHAPTER
SEVEN

WALK AROUND WITH THE VICTIMS, baring it all for the camera.

It isn't worth the effort trying to hack into an account, learning of passwords and various security codes, when you're already so close to the victim, considered a friend, a valued name, someone they recognize, have been talking to for quite some time.

"Quite some time." I love that phrase. Don't you?

Its purpose is to say that it's been a while but not long enough to say "a long time."

Yet how long is "a long time" measured in internet minutes and moments? How long does it really take to make a connection, to understand the difference between true friend and troll, safe zone and danger?

In the family's case, it didn't take very long.

Not when you have at least a few mutual friends.

How long have you been connected?

Excellent. You nudged me out by a few days.

The son accepts all friend requests and followers. It's all about quantity for him. As the son, he undermines his other role, one of being a child, and accentuates his confidence, or lack thereof, via any and all activity.

The wife reveals nothing about her role as mother. Her

profiles remain spare, the lone image being her profile picture. She only accepts requests from people she met via a dating website, where I've found—unsure if you've noticed this too—she is content with a single, initial message before going silent. But I believe we've both gotten past that silence. Yeah, she'll keep talking, like most, if there's something relatable, something she can care about.

The husband denounces his role as father, his accounts maintaining pictures and content from a previous decade. His activity borders on self-referential, which seems to create a retrospective, a performance in and of itself, of his years as an eligible twenty-something bachelor. Like his son, he accepts all friend requests and followers. He'll reply to every comment and message. He'll exaggerate any activity or event, be it work or leisure, in order to help convince himself that he's having a good time.

Interesting to see that without knowing beforehand that each are related, you wouldn't be able to notice, not with their names being altered, the son donning first name and first initial of last name, wife using her maiden name, and husband using an abbreviation of his professional name. They exist to accentuate their alternate roles, wearing masks that conceal the most fragile components of their private lives.

And yet, we've already looked.

And we've already found…

The rest, I'll quote you, "Fills in the blanks."

I want to say that it has become much easier to case a performance since the dawn of new modes of intrusion. It functions the same with their home: When the victim doesn't know of the intrusion, watching from the shadows cast by the trees a couple feet from your front door, when the victim doesn't realize that you're inside his/her house, the camera is able to cast a mold, one that captures a perfect replication of the individual.

You'd look so good on camera.

Cue the first thing I said to the wife:

You'd look so good on camera.

And then—hey, yeah, we were matched by the algorithm. Or something.

Yeah, haha. I dunno how any of it works.

It's probably a crapshoot: randomizes people based on the things they clicked under hobbies.

Yeah, haha. Dating sites are sinkholes of depression.

Yup, that's me.

Then you must be... ha. No, I don't think it's a bad pic. Seriously, yeah.

You should see some of the pics people post.

I don't remember how we became friends though. Guess you friended me, or I friended you. Either way.

I'm bored most days. And I spend way too much time on here.

Haha, you and I are the same. I'm divorced, yeah. Got divorced a month ago. I work from home... which is basically like saying, "I don't know what I'm doing with my life." Haha. It's true though. I don't know what I'm doing. It's like I'm lonely but I don't have it in me to go out and start dating again. I also don't have it in me to find more clients, so I spend a lot of time online, talking to people that I really don't know, doing this basically. I could be a professional stalker.

One of the best. Stalker for hire: I'll make you feel blessed!

Haha. I'm rambling, sorry.

I hit enter after every single line. I don't mean to, but I just can't write paragraphs on here. But then it sounds like I'm blasting you with prompt noises.

Oh, yeah. Thanks. Really though, sorry for rambling. I'm probably not making any sense.

That makes me feel better.

I'm not joking: I spend all day online. I don't leave my laptop for one second.

At least you have a kid to take care of. Only thing I'm taking care of is my budding alcoholism.

Haha. I'm managing but I am tempted to do a little day-drinking.

It goes well with social media.

Tell me a little about yourself. Don't make me guess based on the hobbies you listed. Haha. Oh, come on, you aren't really depressed, are you? You're too silly to be depressed. I used to take that. I stopped after I lost health insurance. Couldn't afford to keep seeing the shrink. Haha. Looks like we're exactly the same. But you have your daughter and your family and stuff... you've got a support network.

Ah, don't say that.

They couldn't really be the reason for your depression.

Seriously?

He's cheating on you?

How long?

Wow—I apologize. That was uncalled for. I don't mean "wow" in any other way than mere shock. I'm shocked.

I know how it feels.

It happened to me too. My ex cheated on me for a whole year before I found out.

It's better that you found out sooner. Believe me.

I know you can't trust me, a stranger, but take it from me: It's so much worse when you find out that it's been happening for such a long time. Yeah, trust me. We've just met but I know I can trust you. Do you trust me?

You can tell me anything.

I know you better than you think.

Did the husband try to hit on you? Let me see the emails.

To: Victim #2

From: Invader #1

Greetings, my colleague and I have reviewed your redaction to our proposal. I understand that we do not have the appropriate specifications for the guest house; however, please consider that our level of understanding is not to meet yours. I, for one, cannot fathom the industry lingo, or what-have-you, incorporated into your "recommended" additions. In fact, I am having difficulty maintaining a professional tone in this email. I've yet to fully explain the reason for my difficulty and I am already not sure I know what I want. I assume your recommendations are mandatory? Might we be able to discuss this over the phone, in plainer terms?

Thank you for your time.

Sincerely,
Invader #1

To: Invader #1

From: Victim #2

I'd be glad to schedule a phone call. What is your line of work? My recommendations are nothing to worry about; I'd be happy to do more of the legwork here. Keep in mind that since this is considered freelance, I will charge by the hour. Not to worry, the juice won't start until we're on the same page. That's my way of using some lingo outside of this stiff and stuffy industry. I will do my best to cut the dense talk out of our conversations!

Victim #2

Address/contact info/credentials

To: Invader #1

From: Victim #2

I enjoyed our talk. I had no idea you were an artist! That's exciting. I envy the more bohemian lifestyles and, please, don't take it as a sign of disrespect. I really do envy people that don't have mortgages, six-figure business loans, and so many responsibilities it makes me feel like I want to jump off a bridge. I kid, I kid, but perhaps there's some truth to this. Lately, I don't know… Well, to switch topics, I have thought it over and, yes, I understand your situation completely. And your offer, I will take it. This project sounds like more fun than anything else I've got going at the moment

Victim #2

To: Victim #2

From: Invader #1

Thank you so much! We're delighted. I enjoyed our talk as well. Sorry about sounding distant, I was on the cell and it makes me sound strange. I'm ecstatic, so ecstatic. My sister (my colleague, it was my attempt at sounding professional) and I have been trying to get this made for our mom for so long. Fact that it's coming true makes you a godsend. Oh and my life isn't all that glamorous. If it wasn't for my sister, I wouldn't be able to pay the bills. You could say I'm lonely too. When you do what I do, there's not a lot of time to pay attention to life. At least your life has some sort of routine. It isn't the same thing every day. Maybe you hate it but at least you have something to come home to. I've got my canvases, my doubts. Ugh, haven't had a project sell for seemingly ages. I've rewritten this email numerous times. Anyway, thank you. I really mean it!

Sincerely,

Invader #1

To: Invader #1

From: Victim #2

No need to thank me. Really, I mean it. It feels good when all this education and "prowess" actually goes towards something. I didn't become an architect to call myself an architect. I found some extra time in the office and I fleshed out the proposal into better form. It is beginning to take on the appearance of a real blueprint! I'll be working over the next couple days on something you can see. I can't, unfortunately, make it to the office over the weekend. I'm obliged to bring the family out to see that new rollercoaster at the whatever you call it, theme park in the city. I can't remember the name. Not important. I will be unable to work on your project even though I really would like to. I mean it. I really do. It's more interesting than most of what's going on in my life right now. You said I'm lucky. I don't know about that. Really, I'm bored. I would like to walk you through the new version—which I've attached to this email. Can I call you this evening? I plan on staying late.

Victim #2

To: Victim #2

From: Invader #1

You can call me anytime! After 8PM that is :). I'm working on a new piece that I think might actually have some potential (read: won't suck). Thanks so much about taking on the project. I think I'm starting to sound like an annoying echo but really, thank you. You're going out of your way to help me and I want you to know that I appreciate it. I wish there was some way I could thank you. I haven't heard about that rollercoaster. I don't get out much, actually. It sounds great though: a family outing. I don't know if I can really raise kids. I haven't been able to even keep a boyfriend for more than three months. I'm envious. I bet your family is great. Anyway, I look forward to your call!

Sincerely,

Invader #1

Did he call?

Of course he did. The story repeats on a different stage.

Yet it isn't his infidelity that demands our attention. Not precisely. You should consider bringing it up at some point during the performance.

How would you like to go about this one? I doubt the son is capable of any surprises. Yup, I agree. Better to lay it out, summarizing wherever necessary.

Pieced together via three different social media accounts and one number purchased and used solely for text messaging, the performance ventured into the roles of three separate people, one local, two the son has never met before. On all accounts, it was an act of catering to the son's interests and ego.

For the majority of mine, the one account I handled, I liked what he posted and occasionally replied with comments like:

"But what does that say about the beer supply?"

"[Celebrity name] is following this post."

"It's all about making hot chicks second guess their hotness."

Whether or not the son noticed my comments or not, you couldn't be sure until, I assume, he noticed the profile picture, remembered the name, looked at some of my own posts, ones that go back more than a week, before messaging me to chat.

During the chat, he talked about music. He talked about his band making it.

He played up the cliché of being a teenage male with disposable cash, capable of buying what he wants, and would go (and did) as far as offering to pay for things since I was a seemingly attractive girl his age, interested in his band, interested in flattery, but mostly interested in what he'll tell me about his family.

I messaged him a few times, mostly late at night.

Angry, about parents, about finals, about the future. The son had a reply. The replies could have been right out of a book on how to say the right thing. The son said the right thing, every time. I noted the other details, the truths hidden within the lines.

To note, then, during the correspondence:

They are going to leave the house at 9AM — "going to have to wake up so fucking early" — and they won't be back until 10PM at the earliest — "mom's going to want to see everything because the 'princess' the 'favorite' will want to see everything and dad's too indifferent to give a shit." We knew this, didn't we? And yet, there's another nugget, one that wasn't expected. The son with a line that could be used for the performance, incorporated into its latter scenes. The son texted, "Want to just hire a bunch of people to kill my parents, destroy the house, so that I get all the insurance money and never have to do anything I don't want ever again. Get to focus on the band."

The son offers a lick of creativity.

It wasn't the first.

Invader #5 donned the role of the second account. She goes to the same high school and, between the two they have twenty mutual friends. It's a good profile picture. Believable. It almost looks like the real person. Almost. And yet, the real person wouldn't want anything to do with the son. The real person doesn't have an account, favoring a profile on another social media service. And yet those that friended this account are the ones that seek her out. They are the ones that have distant interest in her. Invader #5 spent the majority of their chats—which had to be restrained to two or three exchanges at most, since we couldn't have the son assume that they were bonding, becoming friends; that could lead to in-person confrontation. If it happened, it would perturb. It would create suspicion. It wouldn't end up ruining the performance, and yet, it could have derailed our casing. The camera can have all it wants; either way, it'll make it look better than it really was. It'll strip away the cues and other planned orchestrations and it'll show the action—the actuality of each scene, each suggestion.

Invader #5 has changed her hair color, purchased cosmetic eye-color contact lenses, and has begun to embrace everything the son assumes is true about the person.

Invader #5 used the account for casing purposes. The role she will play requires a degree of precedence in order to be effective later. When invader #5 steps into frame, the son will question every single exchange he's had with a person online and in person. It's one of the more enticing and alarming sides to the spectacle.

This is a spectacle, above all. The craft pertains to keeping and maintaining a captive audience; behind the camera, you'll never know how it happened—the trickery that made the impossible possible, the insanity so close to home. It is spectacle.

Using the phone number, I imagine you took advantage anonymity.

It was tiring, yes, but it was necessary because we couldn't garner enough information about the son's habits. He remains in his room. We know that. He is frequently online. We also know that. He is disinterested in the majority of what happens around the house. Also common information. However, we didn't expect him to notice the change in atmosphere, the tension in the house, the dog missing. But he did. Through online activity, the son made it clear that something is happening at home, yet we cannot be certain if he has noticed the camera.

It was the reason why you had to make additional contact. This is about testing victim #4. It's about measuring how he'll react, logic et al.

A list of times you texted and he replied—

7:21AM—"Who is this?"
    7:45AM—"Don't know who she is."
    7:49AM—"Is she cute?"
    7:50AM—"I don't know her."
    7:51AM—"No."
    5:02PM—"Stop it."
    5:55PM—"You're trolling me."
    9:09PM—"I said stop."
    11:27PM—"No."
    11:32PM—"I can just block you."
    11:45PM—"Jesus."
    11:56PM—"Umm."
    12:05AM—"I think I know who this is. You're so damn immature dude."
    12:08AM—"Dude? Lay off it now, okay?"

A list of times you texted and he didn't reply—

5:03PM—"Is she there?"
    5:05PM—"Is she there?"
    8:15PM—"Is she there?"
    11:29PM—"Is she there?"
    11:30PM—"Is she there?"
    11:31PM—"Is she there?"
    11:35PM—"Is she there?"
    11:52PM—"Is she there?"
    11:59PM—"Is she there?"
    12:02AM—"Is she there?"
    12:04AM—"Is she there?"
    12:10AM—"Is she there?"

12:13AM—"Is she there?"
12:18AM—"Is she there?"
12:20AM—"Is she there?"
12:22AM—"Is she there?"
12:24AM—"Is she there?"
12:27AM—"Is she there?"

A victim looks right at the camera. What do they see?
They see themselves in the mirror.
They see themselves itemizing every email and post.
They see themselves for what they're missing.
Yet they don't see what's coming.
They never see what's coming.
A performance well planned and played out is truly a shock. It leaves people frozen in place, unable to process what they just saw. Beginning, middle, and end, the best ones can be viewed as premonitions. As if saying—
"You have a nice home. May I join in?"

The next step of the performance will take place on a Saturday. The camera will pan across the front of a darkened house, the single light found inside coming from a bedroom lamp left on by an invader, not the victims. The camera will cut to a close-up from a window, someone parting the blinds... the wife peering outside, frightened about what she's found.
And it'll be like the tuning of instruments, priming for the first song.
The pulloff begins ten minutes after the family leaves for the amusement park.
The morning of Saturday, May 14th, 20XX.
The cults will be pleased.

"WHO'S WATCHING WHILE YOU WERE AWAY..."

SINGLE FILE, keep close to a crouch. Move on the tips of your toes. It's early but not early enough to keep the hikers and runners from using the trail. You don't want them to see you. If I can see you, anyone can see you. You need to change that. I'm watching from a wide shot; it should be like seeing little dots in the distance, like something that could be confused as dirt on the lens. Don't walk in a group.

Come on now... stick to every preplanned cue.

Use what you've learned from other performances.

Use what you've learned from me.

Use what you've learned via casing.

Use it all, because you've returned.

There's no going back.

At the onset of this, the next step, the pulloff, you scale the brick wall, one by one, invaders in file. The house is as you left it, in a state of understated neglect. Though the family calls it home, it has become the film set of an original performance. The sanctity of privacy has been torn down.

Public and private become synonyms of performance.

You wait.

And wait.

Invaders #1, #2, and #3 crouched behind a slight embankment in the backyard.

Invaders #4 and #5 are ten minutes behind, walking the trail at their own pace. Voice is a dozen miles away, in a motel room, watching what the camera records. Voice waits. He has a much longer wait than most of the crew.

Victims can be seen in the large kitchen window.

Victims #1 and #2 avoid looking at each other, the distress of marriage clearly visible. Victims #3 and #4 can't be seen from the window.

Victim #3 runs out into the backyard. She does a few cartwheels.

She turns and shouts at someone off-camera, "Let's go! Let's go! We're going to be the last people there!"

Victim #2 steps out into the lawn, gaze fixed on the daughter, "Did you go the bathroom? Once we're off, we're not stopping."

Victim #3 nods.

Victim #2 takes in the view of the backyard. She pauses on the embankment, as if suddenly aware of your presence, aware of the role she never accepted much less auditioned for, and it's that moment, this moment right now, that makes these sorts of performances so ominous. Victim #2 as wife and mother glimpses a scene down the line.

It's a moment that passes by, forgotten, pushed aside.

But you saw it didn't you?

You saw what the camera saw: She saw you. She felt your presence.

Subconsciously it registered as real. The threat, the danger, the feeling of being watched... Victim #2 will likely be preoccupied for the entire day, not that it's anything new. Instead of engaging with this omen, the moment passes and victim #2 joins victim #1 on the walk to the garage. In silence, they load up the vehicle.

Victim #1 pulls out of the driveway.

This is the first time you notice victim #4. We can assume that he had been sitting in the car, sulking the entire time.

The gate opens and closes. And they're gone.

Wait a couple minutes until invaders #4 and #5 reach the brick wall.

Tell them to wait. You have to go in first.

Enter through the basement, vantage point #2, and tell invader #2 to tend to the circuitry, the heater, the technical details, while invader #3 and you venture upstairs.

The camera can see you through the windows, capturing a wide-angle shot of two figures in black. Yeah, you tend to stick out in daylight. Yet by nightfall, you'll be as close to blending in with the night as possible.

You should be okay.

No one's looking. Well, no one but the cults and your crew.

Double check that all security devices are disengaged.

Use the default manufacturer codes on the garage panel. Same goes with the security system. Better to tend to it now, before occupying your time with the more creative endeavors. You should carry all the materials you need to vantage point #3. From there, few will look. There's a tendency to disregard the kids' room as a location where intruders may be hiding, and it's precisely the reason why you should accentuate this fact.

Invader #3 joins you and invader #2 in the daughter's room.

Sliding open the closet door, you see that the crawlspace will be more than enough for all the necessary tools. This is a good sign.

I was under the impression that you might not fit some of the items.

Yeah, I understand. It's funny now when we look back, but hiding in there, yeah, I bet it was rough. You do it for the craft, for the sake of the performance.

All the items safely stowed, you can get on to the last canvassing of the house.

Systematic walkthrough, room-by-room, all three of you taking to one corner, moving outward in concentric circles.

I see that you have your crew wearing gloves.

Do you plan on repeat performances?

It's all going according to plan.

Infiltration by way of the backup crew begins with them climbing over the brick wall, stepping through the rickety fence, and tending to the neighbors.

You didn't see that coming, but then again, I told you:

Half of the performance is improvisation.

I picked them out for a reason.

They've done this before. Not this particular type of performance, no. Yet they did this numerous times before. For financial gain. No, it wasn't about the craft in any of the previous cases. Invaders #4 and #5 have a history of robbery and assorted crimes. I trust them. You will too. They have their plan all figured out. It fills in the idle moments during the performance, when they're not needed. I recommend that you use the end-result of the neighbor's house as a possible red herring, something to confuse the authorities, maybe something that'll send them down the wrong trail.

Creativity. The performance excels when it takes drastic and unexpected turns.

Turn on the lamp in the master's bedroom. It won't burn out. It has to be that one. It's the one that can be seen from the street. The way the window is positioned, the way the curtains are thin, translucent, and the blinds incapable of hiding the shape and arrangement of the room, lends itself perfectly to the first indication that something is wrong. And it will be seen. The family will pull in and it'll be victim #2 that notices the light. It will be victim #2 that turns off the lamp.

It will be victim #2 that peeks through the blinds and sees invader #3 in position, as intended, waving back at her from just inside the gate.

Set up the television so that it plays what the camera sees.

Yeah, it'll run all night. No sound. It'll only distract.

It'll be interesting to see how long it takes before one of the victims notice.

It's about 3PM. The lull has begun. Tools in place, initial inspection complete, you're starting to get anxious. I bet you're a little nervous too. Yeah, it's normal. This is going to happen; you can't avoid nerves.

Sit at the kitchen table.

Relax for a moment.

Pretend that it's your home. This is your house.

Imagine yourself as the victims.

Tap into what I said about fear. What do you fear? Back into the master bedroom. Yes—great idea.

Pick an outfit out of the wife's closet. Something formal. No, not that dress. How about that one? Yeah, that's the one. It'll do nicely. Lay it out neatly on the bed.

Now go into the husband's closet. That's a nice suit, lay it out next to the dress.

Do the same for the daughter. A little Sunday dress.

The son's going to dress up for the occasion. He'll wear the only suit he has. On the bed, yeah. Get your partners to bring up the dead dog.

You'll want it to stink up the foyer a bit. Give it time to really permeate through the house. Now see about where you can hide. Not just vantage points. You'll need a sequence of blind spots, corners, crawlspaces, and other locations for both you and the other invaders. I can't tell you where exactly because you could be anywhere. In theory, I shouldn't be able to see you either. If the camera doesn't see it, no one will.

Look for those kinds of places.

It starts to get dark around 6PM. Everything's going according to plan.

The place is starting to smell.

Remove one mask and play the role of another. In this case, it's a physical mask being removed but mostly to clear the sweat dripping profusely down the front of your face. You could try face paint but that might run too.

Where are your partners?

Look at the television.

Find out.

Invader #2 is playing guitar in the son's room.

Invader #3 is sitting in the treehouse, vantage point #1, smoking a cigarette.

He looks nervous.

You are at the kitchen table, thinking about what else to do before it happens. If you get nervous, just remember that it has already begun. This is merely the next in a long series of scenes. Scene after scene, there's a new kick, a new curiosity, but you shouldn't worry so much. You're supposed to enjoy this.

This: The calm before the storm.

That's not a good hiding spot. Think clearer, places where victims will look. Now take those—behind closed doors, cabinets, closets, behind curtains or furniture—and do the opposite. Yeah. I'm just fucking with you. Be more creative. Think in shadows, and then use those shadows. Walk in silent step. When something makes a sound, you want it to be because you or your partners made that sound.

And you'll get used to the smell.

Victim #4 posts a number of times on his social media accounts while at the amusement park. Looking through, it's mostly negative stuff—having to wait for two and a half hours in line for the rollercoaster, the new one, the reason for going in the first place, and how they all took turns standing in line, swapping out when one needed to go to the bathroom, or to get some food—but there's also information about the family's ETA. They will be here a little later, if only because victim #1 promised victim #3 they'd stop by a certain restaurant for chocolate chip pancakes before arriving home.

Much to the dismay of victim #2 and #4.

Victim #1 at it again—doing his best to dolt it out so that he remains somewhat relevant in his daughter's life.

If you plan on using the restroom, keep it loose and mellow; don't drop any loads and keep it straight liquid. This is imperative. You don't want to leave behind any trace.

The voice is in transit. He will arrive late in the night, approximately an hour after the family returns, which had originally been two hours after they returned home. The slight change affects nothing. Keep things on track.

Call him now. You want the voice to tend to an important part of the performance. You and the rest of your crew have too much else to take care of. You cannot tend to phone calls while you are leading and linking victims' actions into creative consequences. Let him know. I didn't think you would be the one to do it.

It's okay—this is why I am here. Guidance for when you need it. And just as often when you don't. I know. Not very funny. Remember: Put yourself in their position.

The house has an intercom system integrated into every single room. The master control is in the kitchen. Might as well play some music. Fire up something. Let it echo throughout the house. Set up the intercom so that you can communicate with both partners and victims.

Wouldn't you find it frightening to hear partners talk to each other while you, the would-be victim, hid under the bed or locked yourself in a closet?

The camera loves that brand of suspense.

Invaders #4 and #5 have neutralized the neighbors.

Both children bound and gagged but otherwise unharmed. They have been locked in the basement with the deceased father. Mother remains unconscious and tied up, just in case you may need a decoy. Think of it as something left for possible spoilage.

Did you move the body into the vent? You'll want to make it somewhat difficult to find. It will allow for victims to meander, linger around, free roam while you track them, designing the next scene.

Invader #3 does not know how to dance. He really shouldn't be out of character. Tell him to stop. It's embarrassing.

Better to play house than to dance to horrible pop music. I don't know how you can listen to that stuff. Well, even if it isn't you that chose to listen to it… ugh. Anyway, time for a dry run. I'm talking first rounds, how it'll all initially unfold.

Everything should be set.

Everything that can be preplanned that is.

Assign roles for the dry run.

You don the mask of victim #1.

Invader #2 dons the mask of victim #2.

Invader #3 dons the mask of victim #3.

Victim #4 can be disregarded given what will happen to him shortly after commencement.

Victim #1 parks the car. He's tired and regretting eating that food. But he's trying to make his daughter happy. He hasn't spoken at all to his wife.

Victim #4 his son is forgotten in the backseat.

Victim #1 thinks about that freelance project and more so the woman artist he's been corresponding with via email. He is the first to enter the house and, as he turns the doorknob, it hits him.

That smell. What the hell is it?

Invader #3 says something like, "Eww what is that?"

Invader #2 is silent.

Inside the house, he notices that he forgot to turn on the security system. Wrong—he did but then again, he hasn't met the rest of the cast yet.

He is too busy with the smell.

The son presumably wanders into the kitchen to steal a beer. Invader #2 breaks away from the family and goes up the stairs.

Invader #2 turns right at the top of the stairs. Tell him his other right. He went the wrong direction. Right. There you go. Invader #2 goes into the master bedroom and maybe notices the clothes laid out for the performance. Maybe not.

What's more important is that lamp.

It means everything and nothing.

It means something is indeed happening.

This is the first scene.

Now invader #2 walks over to the window.

Much like that morning in the backyard, when victim #2 stopped and seemed to pick up on something, a would be omen if she hadn't let go of the thought before it could manifest itself as true, victim #2 stops at the window, places a hand on one of the blinds and parts it slowly. Victim #2 will inhale, hold her breath, and peek through the parting.

She will expect to see someone waving back, almost as if it's a fantasy, one that she dreamt about frequently, the kind used with make-believe, the sort of pretend that the silence of the suburbs will undoubtedly encourage. Because it won't actually happen.

Because it isn't really like that. It won't happen to you.

Thoughts presenting themselves before seeing it happen. She'll see it happen. She might even wave back. But it won't hit her as reality until she's walking over to the bed, reaching for the dress we chose.

It'll be right then and there that it clicks.

She begins to understand her role in the performance.

The camera will zoom in close, holding the shot as fear begins to form. First, it's the edges of her mouth twitching, then her lip quivering, the creases on her forehead defining the alarm. And then she sees the camera.

If only for one instant, she sees it.

And then it's gone.

Playing house sets the mood. It sets the tone. Calm those nerves. The minute hand is inching toward 11PM. The voice is hiding in the bushes. He's here way too early. Tell him to go to vantage point #1. Tell him not to be stupid and hide in the fucking treehouse. Get into positions. Don the right mask, the one you'll wear the most.

Victims on the horizon…

Behind the camera you can bet the cults will be clamoring for the next scene, on the edge of their seats, hoping for this performance to meet their expectations. Think about how the cults will react, when the see the record.

Think about what you should do and then think about how to break out of that routine. You'll be breaking more than routines tonight.

Starting positions—

Invader #1 upstairs in the daughter's room, vantage point #3.

Invader #2 down in the basement, vantage point #2.

Invader #3 in the shadows near the garage, vantage point #3. Upon lamp being turned off, invader #3 will wander up to the front lawn, gaze up to the designated window. And the wave, slow and deliberate, the mask evident and obvious of malicious intent, blurred out to prevent any and all details besides that.

Voice in the treehouse, waiting and smoking.

Invaders #4 and #5 watch from the windows of the neighbor's house. Lights on, illusion of a comfortable night at home.

Turn off all the lights. Turn off the music. The gate opens.

Enter the family. The lone light source being the vehicle's headlights casting a caustic beam across the lightless house, windows blank, everything inside quiet and hushed; the image is alarming to those that know. To the right viewer, it is ominous. It's an open grave waiting for someone walking by to trip and fall in.

Sound of doors slamming shut.

A close-up of each victim's face before they make the walk towards the house. It's the first beat of the scene. It's the first time you'll really get to say hello. It's the first time you'll be able to let them know we've been here the entire time, watching.

In the family room, the television plays back the scene unfolding upstairs in the master's bedroom. If the other victims stopped to watch, they'd know too what the wife discovers from the onset. But I think it's smart that you set it up so that they find out later.

Victim #2, the most fragile of the entire family, knows first and is the last to say anything about the camera.

Everything's going according to plan.

CHAPTER
NINE

POSITIONS, everyone's in position. A moment of hushed silence and awe as the camera pans through the darkened corridors of the house, following victim #1 and victim #3 as they seek out the source of the smell. They seek out a particular sound, the sound of central air pushing the bulk of the dead dog's body against the grating.

Victim #2 seated watching the television. She watches the camera watching her husband and daughter walk through the house.

Voice is still in the treehouse. Make sure to keep him off camera until his cue. It'll be tempting to call on his aid earlier than usual. Don't. In doing so, he'll become just another invader. He walks a fine line that must remain as barely visible as possible.

Invaders #2 and #3 are at vantage point #1.

They've met up and have begun with preparations.

You shouldn't move yet.

Give the camera it's moment. Angled low, you see two sets of feet, walking and pausing, the hunt for the stench becomes the opening reveal:

Victims #1 and #3 discover the body pressed against one of the larger vents in the kitchen.

I imagine you'll stick to the second floor. Yeah, it's a precarious situation to be in. Though you understand what needs to happen, you have a tenuous hold on the current thread of the performance. It's all camera angles and buildup. It's all about the victims, you see? At this juncture, the crew must pull back to allow for the alarm to be seen from the victims' perspective. Up until this point, the focus of the performance has been placed on you, the invader as lead, as star, of sorts, and it's about time that things take a back seat to the discover, the brewing of concern, the eerie torment that any good performance does for those that know of its inevitable gruesome conclusion.

The family needs to wear their roles effectively.

Give them time to fit in the palm of your hand.

Only then can you clench your fist to smother.

Victim #1 deals with the discovery by—first—staring blankly at the body and then—second—covering his daughter's eyes with his right hand. Too late, it seems, because victim #3 has seen what he's seen.

"Sshh," victim #1 says.

Victim #1 positions himself in front of the body, edging out victim #3, who does her best to push through, to see what he shouldn't let her young mind see.

Victim #1 shouts at victim #4, "Get your sister out of here!"

Victim #4 does his best to remain unfazed, "Yeah, whatever." #3 and #4 leave the kitchen. Victim #1 crouches down next to the body.

"Fuck," he mutters.

What must he be thinking? There are a number of possibilities here. Beyond any and all suspicion, it's a simple case of how. How did this happen? The cults already know, much like victim #2 already knows. And yet, you have to think about what goes on in his head. At this moment, it's the mere sight of the body causing him to freeze. One whole extended sequence of victim #1 in a crouch, palm covering his lips.

Victim #1 was unaware of the dog's disappearance.

He looks into the vent, camera over his shoulder to get a

look at some of the fluid that dripped from the body onto the metal grating.

It's working. Victim #1 inspects the fluid. Processing one thought and then the other, leading to the fact that the body is no longer fresh.

Touching the body releases foul gases, causing him to retch.

"Jesus Christ," he stands up. Exhaling deeply, he walks towards the sink, washing his hands twice. You know what's funny? If he were to look outside right now, he'd see invader #2 moving across the lawn, towards the other side of the wall dividing this house and the next. However, victim #1 is too preoccupied with the situation.

No leads other than something isn't right.

He hasn't connected the dots yet.

He hasn't thought about the security system. Then again, how often do you think of something malicious when you notice that the security system is off? Perhaps I would and so would you, but we're far more aware of these triggers. Victim #1 has forgotten on a number of occasions. Tonight's failure is yet another.

You kind of feel for the guy, though. Despite the performance, victim #1 is oblivious to the facts. You're not seeing it yet but believe me, the cults have it good.

We're warming up.

After he washes his hands, he stands in the kitchen, stunned look on his face. Camera gets a good shot of it. He doesn't know what to do.

Victim #1 digs through the cupboard. He retrieves a box of garbage bags.

Yeah, I see what he's doing there. Give him some credit: Perhaps he's understood that there's nothing else to be done. The body needs to go. The longer he waits, the worse it gets. Victim #1 uses one trash bag per hand, wrapping the plastic in layers like a glove. He reaches down and flips the body over. Victim #1 turns his head away from the body, gagging, "Oh god."

Victim #1 makes another attempt, but the body is too heavy for him to lift and wrap it with plastic. He calls the son's name.

The son's name is muffled. The camera doesn't pick it up. Victim #4 walks in, "What?"

"What do you think?!" He holds up the bag, "Help me here."

Victim #3 remains in the other room, crying.

Victim #2 watches, on the television, the husband and son fumble and gag as they wrap the body in five garbage bags. Somehow, bearing witness to conflict is easier when viewed from behind the camera.

Upon discovering the dead body of her beloved pet, victim #3 breaks down into tears. I'm all about considering first thoughts, those first impressionable thoughts. She took it well. Better than most. There are tears, yes. Look at those tears.

You're not seeing this. That's right.

Those in charge of this performance must be all in or get the hell out. You'll begin to understand how perfect of a scene this is after you've met the family firsthand, seen their puffy eyes, bloodshot, their bodies sunken and wilting under the pressures of their roles. Wearing their masks, they will show you how a victim reacts to the camera's every command whether they recognize the cue or not.

Victim #3 holds onto #4's hand, gripping hard.

Victim #4 tells her, "It'll… be okay." The sheer insincerity of it causes her to drop to the hardwood floor, balling up with her face buried inside her arms and knees.

In the foyer, she remains. The tears begin to envelope her fears.

It sounds as though she forces the tears, the whimpering, the emotional fallout when in fact, the daughter peers down the hall when victim #4 is called back into the kitchen by victim #1. The daughter is curious. It is here that we witness an interesting counterpoint to her otherwise innocence-born naivety.

Her role continues to be the one with the most potential to evolve over the course of the performance.

Victim #2 watches the daughter cry on the television. Somehow, bearing witness to conflict is easier when viewed from behind the camera.

Right from the start, victim #4 establishes his emotional distance by looking away, choosing to ignore what victim #1 pulls out of the vent. He walks over to the kitchen table and sits down in front of victim #2's laptop.

He signs in under guest and checks his email.

He clicks around, deleting old emails when he discovers that he has nothing new waiting for him. He checks his social media accounts, eyes narrowing when victim #3 starts to cry. The camera pans in close on the screen as victim #4 scrolls through his news feed. He has no interest in feeling vulnerable and so victim #4 chooses to feel nothing.

He denies the fear and will continue to do so, probably until it's already too late to do anything about it. I should mention that there's always one victim that does a one-eighty. During the spoilage section, there's a character that becomes the thorn in your side, the one that tries to take a steak knife and stab it in your kidney. But victim #4 isn't the one to do it. I've seen a number of performances and it might be that you'll have to tend to the spoilage all by yourself. I'm not quite sure yet. However, it won't be the son. I should clarify: It could be the son but if he continues to smother and deny, he'll be the meekest of the four, the one victim that you kill off just because you have to set an example. So, take that for whatever it's worth:

Victim #4, to be used as an example.

If and when the time comes.

If he switches masks and becomes the one that I thought he might be, I'd go with… oh, I don't know. #1. The father?

Give it some thought.

Victim #2 watches the son smother his emotions, holding back what should have been an all-encompassing shiver. Somehow, bearing witness to conflict is easier when viewed from behind the camera.

Victim #2 is malleable. You'll be able to use her to signal the rest of the family because she'll be unable to express anything but the baseline, the simplest warning or idea. She watches it all unfold and yet you cannot help but see that the information passes right through, barely registering. The lamp, the wave, the curious omen that might have caused a drastic change in the performance concluded in her dismissal of what's happening. Drowning in the haze of her depression, she's forgotten by the family, sitting there on the couch, frozen in place.

Victim #2 watches herself on television. Somehow, bearing witness to conflict is easier when viewed from behind the camera.

Hey, tell invaders #2 and #3 to get into position. What are they doing? You have to make sure every partner stays on track. Now's not the time to be smoking cigarettes in the shadows. You should care. So what if they're going to follow through? So what if they cannot be seen by the family?

You cannot afford to make any mistakes until you're within grip of the victims.

They could always call the authorities right then and there.

Maintain the right camera angle and they'll follow each invisible cue.

They talk about what to do. Indeed, what do you do with the dog now? Victim #1 shakes his head, "No, not that." He doesn't want to move it.

Victim #4 shrugs, "Well you're going to have to fucking do something."

Victim #1 frowns, "Don't you talk to me like that." He sighs, looks up at his son and then reaches into his pocket.

"What?"

"Shut up," victim #1 says.

He dials a number. No, not that number. It's more than three digits.

The camera picks up the ringing it's so quiet.

On the sixth ring, someone picks up.

"Hello?" victim #1 says after he doesn't hear another voice on the line.

Then a woman's voice, "Hey…"

Victim #1 says, "Umm, I-I don't know why I called… I guess I didn't know who else to call. Umm…"

"What's wrong…?"

He looks up at the son, "Well…"

The details are given: Dead dog. Found in vent. Strange.

The son adds, "It went missing."

"Hmm?"

"The dog," #4 points at the body, "it went missing like a day ago."

Victim #1 looks over at the body, sighs, "'She.'"

"What?"

"'It's' a 'she.' You shouldn't refer to your pet like it's an object."

Mention of the dog's disappearance.

"I guess I'm asking, then… did you notice anything strange, maybe the dog digging around your yard, maybe she was hurt and got into the vents somehow."

Victim #1 reaches for some sort of explanation.

There's got to be an explanation.

You can hear the line echo out for extra impact.

There always is.

#1's not going to like it…

"I didn't see anything." You can hear the sound of a woman's voice from the phone's receiver. The woman, the neighbor next door.

"Oh, okay, well then…" he trails off, gaze fixed to the dead body. "Take care." There's movement from the hall, "No—get back in the other room!" To the son, he says, "I told you to keep her away from this!"

Victim #3 hides around the corner. Victim #4 makes a face and walks over to the daughter. He whispers, "Just humor him."

Victim #3's eyes are large, puffy, face flush red from crying. She pleads, "We have to bury her."

"Let me and dad do it." The way victim #4 stresses the word "dad" tells us that the son not only dislikes his father but also loathes the man. He glances over at the couch, noticing for the first time, victim #2 frozen in place, watching the television.

Victim #4 rolls his eyes, disappointed.

Victim #3 tugs on #4's shirtsleeve, "I want to say a prayer."

He looks at her, then back at #1. "Fine."

The camera pans around victims #1, #3, and #4.

#4 holds #3's hand, "Just let her."

#1 has his eyes closed, massaging his forehead with his left hand, phone held in his right, "Fine. All right. Fine. Help me with the body."

He sets down the cellphone on the kitchen counter.

Victim #3 watches as #1 and #4 cradle the wrapped body between them, #1 holding the head while #4 holds onto the hind legs.

They shuffle forward, walking around to the door near the laundry room, the one leading out to the porch and, beyond that, the backyard.

Victim #3 runs over to her mother and says, "Mom, we're going to bury her."

Nothing. Not so much as a blink.

"Mom…"

Victim #1's voice can be heard, "Sweetie, can you grab the shovel from the closet. The one where I keep all the gardening equipment?!"

Victim #3's attention is redirected to the new task, "Yeah dad."

She runs down the hall, off camera.

That was close. One extra puff of the cigarette translates to a handful of seconds lost. It only takes one second to derail the momentum. They were a sliver of a second away from crossing paths with victims #1 and #3. If they waited another second… done. Found out.

This is a performance. Your partners need to keep up.

You are supposed to be nervous and anxious.

Invaders #4 and #5 have already improvised—the call to the neighbor, that took a threat and #5 holding a weapon against the woman's throat.

You need to keep in mind that it's all cues. No matter how much of it is planned, none of it exists until it happens and is caught on camera.

None of it exists until you actually do it.

I hate to lecture again but you need to understand. You do, don't you?

Good.

Victim #1 will wish he hadn't left the phone on the kitchen counter.

Anyway, you ready? If it works right, it'll be quite the sight.

Don't you worry about the camera not getting the best take; it always gets the best take. The best take is the one that's recorded. Get it?

You talk to your partners yet?

They lock the doors?

Excellent.

It's time to bring victim #2 up to speed.

We can't have her stunned all night.

It's going to be a long night.

Victim #1 lets the daughter choose where to bury their beloved pet. The body remains near the camera. Victim #2 watches from the couch, the camera set to night-vision for the first time to capture them in the darkness of the unlit backyard following victim #3 as she remains indecisive for a period of time. Inevitably, victim #3 chooses a space near the treehouse. You better tell voice to keep his mouth shut. He makes one wrong move, shifting of his weight causing the wood of the treehouse to creak, taking another puff of a cigarette, or something embarrassing like coughing, and it's going to unravel in mere minutes. You'll be running spoilage right from the start. You might still get a good performance out of this, but it'll lack balance. It won't be a success. So you better make sure your relative keeps quiet. He wasn't supposed to get here so early.

Victims #1 and #4 retrieve the body and commence with digging.

Camera follows from behind.

The ground is hard and dry, causing them some difficulty.

Victim #1 is the first to give up. Victim #4 says something like, "Big surprise," neither #1 nor #3 hears him. In fact, if it weren't for the camera maintaining a close-up shot of the hole-in-progress, it wouldn't have been caught at all.

Victim #4 is much better at digging, throwing some muscle into each thrust of the shovel into the ground.

Victim #1 watches with his arms crossed.

Victim #3 stares back at the house, perhaps not wanting to see the dead body.

Victim #2 remains inside with you and the other invaders. Time to make your move.

Vantage point #3, the daughter's bedroom. You wander over to the light switch. You flick it on and walk up to the window facing the backyard.

You stand there, a figure in silhouette.

It's a wonderful shot.

Victim #3 looks up, attracted to the illuminated window.

And then it happens: exactly what you wanted.

The daughter screams, a perfect blood-curdling pitch.

Switch off the light before father or brother can see.

Get downstairs with invaders #2 and #3.

Make sure the doors are locked. Every single door.

With one bold move, you've made contact.

Voice sits in the treehouse and doesn't make so much as a sound.

Everyone's become a part of the performance now.

"WHAT IS IT, SWEETIE? IS SOMETHING WRONG...?"

THE INFRASTRUCTURE of privacy ends tonight. Victim #1 won't believe it when the daughter tells him that she saw something. Victim #3 explains what she saw: shapes, or rather one shape. People, or rather a person, watching. A person in her room. A person inside the house. A person that couldn't be anyone she knows. A person with a face that... a face that... She deals in splintered thoughts, speaking in panicked gasps. She's so afraid that she cannot begin to cry. Victim #2 shivers. She wraps her arms around her body and shivers. Victim #1 hugs the daughter, "Easy now. It's okay... it's okay."

Her eyes are shut. It is not okay.

"What is it sweetie?"

Victim #3 shakes her head, "No."

The camera captures something. It's worry. Victim #1 is worried.

Victim #3 won't open her eyes.

She's too afraid to open them. Another shiver.

"Sweetie, I'm worried about you."

And then you hear it, what victim #3 had been trying to say:

"I saw him in my room."

Victim #1 has everything to lose. You can see it on his face. He's as afraid as the daughter but the difference here is that he doesn't want to admit it. Victim #4 is willing to believe anything. He's staring up at the daughter's bedroom window.

Lightless, you're already downstairs. Invader #2 walks past one of the kitchen windows.

Victim #4 catches a glimpse. In barely a whisper, "Dad…"

Victim #3 says, "He's still in my room."

"Dad…"

"Sweetie…"

Victim #3 shakes her head, "No."

"Come on now, sweetie, let's go back inside and—"

"No!" That wasn't the daughter. Victim #4 takes a step back, "They're inside…"

The night vision captures the frightened look on all of their faces.

"Do you believe me now?" The daughter sits down in the grass. "No," she pushes away from victim #1.

"I'm not going back in there. Fuck that," says victim #4.

Victim #1 tells him otherwise.

"You can't make us. We got to call the cops."

Victim #1 breaks down, face red. He wipes the sweat from his brow, "I left the phone in the house."

Victim #4 stares back, in disbelief.

He says it again, "I left the phone back in the house…" Victim #1 looks over at the house, its lightless second floor windows.

The kitchen ominous, deserted, until both #1 and #4 see him. They don't realize it's you this time and not invader #2. You walk by one of the windows.

Stop. Stop right now. Yeah, make it look like you know that they're watching.

Good, now look at them.

Take a step towards the window.

This is a great shot. Arms at your sides. Wear that mask. Warm up to the role. Now look over at victim #2. Perfect.

They understand. They're putting together the pieces. They're going to have to step back inside. Walk towards the wife.

The camera pans across their faces.

It's the daughter that says what they're all thinking, "Mom's inside."

She screams, "Mom!"

Victim #1 looks at the daughter, mouth agape, a tear running down his face.

Victim #4 runs towards the house, "Mom…" Victim #1 calls out his name but only a shrill, cracking noise escapes his mouth. Victim #3 starts crying, "Mommy."

After trying the door, victim #4 turns around slowly. He looks at victim #1.

He doesn't need to say anything.

Victim #1 says to no one in particular, "Oh no."

Victim #2 watches her husband, son, and daughter burying their pet. She watches three men wearing all black, faces not quite the sort of face you'd expect to see. She watches three men watch her before disappearing into the darkness of a different room in the house. She blinks and you are gone. Somehow, bearing witness to conflict is easier when viewed from behind the camera.

You are gone, up the stairs, down the hall, digging into the basement for time. Outside, the family warms up to their roles as victims. Inside, the wife blinks, staring at herself on the television, the camera up close, recording her blank expression.

Next door they're dialing victim #1's cellphone. It's invader #4.

Invader #5 talks to the bound and beaten wife like they're best friends.

She talks about her sex life.

She shoots the shit. She has fun, the same kind of fun you'll have soon.

Nothing's happening over at the other house.

The phone's ringing. It's time for victim #2's wakeup call.

This happens while the rest of the family are outside, digging a hole. Victim #2 misses the first call but leaves the couch, walking over to the phone on the kitchen counter in time to pick up the fifth call.

"Hello?"

Nothing. Invader #4 won't say anything at first. He hangs up.

She returns to the television, leaving the phone where it was on the counter.

Ten minutes pass. Another phone call.

"Hello?" This time #2 shows more concern, "Say something."

Invader #4 hangs up.

This time she brings the phone with her.

It rings ten minutes later.

She looks at the screen. It's an unlisted number. Oh, it's just one of those phones you can buy prepaid from a pharmacy somewhere. They got a bunch, like three, to use over the course of the performance. Just in case you'll need one.

Victim #2 lets this one go.

Another ten minutes pass.

Another call. She's confused more than afraid.

The same blank stare from before has been replaced by a curious look. The question here is not—what's going on? Victim #2 understands what's going on. The question here is—what does the camera want?

But the victims don't answer any of the questions. That's for you, and your partners-in-performance, to proclaim.

You'll have to get her to respond.

She picks up the phone, this time she doesn't say anything. Invader #4 plays back the sound of her voice, a recording of her saying, "Say something."

She listens.

The phrase is repeated:

Say something.

Say something.

Say something.

Say something.

Every single time it's altered, sped up a little, using the recording device invader #4 holds up to the receiver.

Invader #4 hangs up.

This time he doesn't wait the ten minutes. He calls back immediately.

Victim #2 doesn't pick up.

After six rings, invader #4 hangs up.

Calls back.

Six rings.

Hangs up.

This repeats a series of times, the only sound in the house being victim #1's ringtone, a slightly altered version of the classic ring.

She hits ignore.

Invader #4 calls again, this time hanging up after the second ring.

When the phone rings again, she chooses to block the number.

Invader #4 moves to the next prepaid phone. He waits a full twelve minutes, enough time to create the illusion that the calls will stop. I would have preferred that he wait until the rest of the family returns but, never mind.

He calls, a different number.

Victim #2 drops the phone, startled.

She leaves the couch, walking towards the foyer.

She peeks into the front yard. Seeing nothing of interest, she walks over to the security system and arms it. It looks like she forgot all about the rest of the family.

Invader #2 visits the garage, pilfering the phone from the wife's purse. While you're at it, you might as well eliminate their laptops, victim #1's desktop PC, and where's victim #4's phone? Yeah, shit—it's probably in his pocket. There's little doubt that it won't have enough battery power left to last more than another half hour.

Keep that in mind though. You don't want any early disturbances.

What's this now?

If there's any doubt about the performance, think less about how it should be, and more about what it's going to be. Think about what needs to happen in order for the cults to favor this performance over hundreds of others. You've got to do something fresh, or really as fresh as it can be before someone steals your idea. But maybe that's enough validation—someone agreed with your actions, your choices. They mimic your own, and in doing so, another performance honors this performance.

It's a good thing. You want the performance to stand on its own two feet. I'm telling you not to worry so much about imitation. So what if that just happened? The camera caught it so it's evidently worthwhile.

Hmm?

I thought it was great.

Check out the footage if you need convincing.

There's a dialog sequence between father and son, #1 and #4. It comes right out of any other performance. It's almost as if a sequence of this type is mandatory. As if it's code.

A version of this sequence has occurred in every single performance worth a damn. It's great to see it delivered so well. I think it's worth something, yes. It happens in most performances because, when fears are on high, it doesn't matter how close you are to calling the cops, running away, or simply hiding somewhere and waiting it out:

You begin to worry about the things you own.

You begin to worry about how this invasion is personal.

It isn't merely an attack on your privacy; it's an attack on your **home**.

If you have no stake in what's in the house, your home, you can just leave. It's that simple. But there's a house full of stuff. It's full of stuff that matters to the victims. More than that, their lives are mapped to those rooms, those furnishings, those pictures, those pairings. So that's why the conversation happens.

That's why the camera caught it, every single word.

It had to happen at one point.

#1 denying #4.

#1 forcing #3 up to her feet.

The main reason being #2.

Mom. Wife.

She's inside.

With an undeclared enemy.

Give it a view. Sit down and watch it played back on the television. They're outside fighting. You have time. They won't be going anywhere.

Victim #1 walks up to the locked door, "What the hell."

Victim #4 shrugs, "It's… locked. It's locked dad."

"Your mother…"

"It's not mom."

Victim #3 hasn't moved. This frustrates #1. He wanders over, picks her up. She fights him off, screaming, slapping at the father, "No! No! No! No! No!" She doesn't want to go back inside.

"She's afraid, dad."

"Fucking hell she's afraid."

Victim #4 raises his voice, "Don't talk to her like that!"

Victim #1 looks his son in the eye, "We're going back in there."

"What, so they can kill us?"

Victim #1 slaps his son. He narrows his eyes, "Don't you ever say that again."

Victim #4 isn't going take that. "Let her go! Don't be an idiot dad. You're such a fucking idiot!"

Victim #1 isn't listening. He's fumbling with the locked door. He kicks at it, muttering profanity under his breath. He's thinking about breaking the door down. He's angry because he's been placed in an uncomfortable position. Victim #1 is afraid. He deals with it in anger.

Victim #4 says, "I'm going to the neighbors and calling the cops. I'm taking her with me. You're going to get her killed."

Victim #1 won't let go of the daughter's hand, "You're not going anywhere."

Victim #4 says, "This happens every single time. Dad, fucking think about it, all right? When something like this happens," the son exhales, suddenly out of breath, "when something like this happens, it's a stupid decision like this that makes it all go to shit. Like absolute shit dad. We can go over there," he points in the direction, "be smart, not end up like everyone else that becomes a part of something like this, and we can get help."

Victim #1 isn't listening. He lets go of the daughter's hand and drives his shoulder into the bulk of the door.

A muted thump, but the door doesn't budge.

"Dad!"

Victim #3 runs over to #4 and hides behind him.

Victim #4 says, "Don't be another victim!"

But it's too late.

It's always too late.

Victim #1 says more or less what everyone says, "I'm not letting them take our home!" It's personal. It's always personal, see? So what if this sequence is derivative. It happens every single time because rational thinking is clouded when the very foundation of your life, everything that's supposed to keep you whole, keep you cognizant of your identity in this society, is invaded by the unknown. It could be a robbery. It could be something more sinister. When it happens to someone, it doesn't matter if it's one or the other. As far as victim #1 is concerned, it's everything.

He thinks about the wife.

He thinks about his life.

He thinks about the safe with his investments, everything of value.

He thinks about his computer, all the sensitive files just waiting to be stolen.

He thinks about their deceased pet, and it's the dog that sends him barreling towards the door again, for the seventh and last strike.

The security system goes off, but it dies out long before anyone notices. In a rural environment, nobody does anything when they hear the sound. They wait a minute or two to see if it stops. It's in that one minute that everything matters.

You move in for the next planned action.

It needs to happen in a single instant.

Under the cover of the disruption, the blaring alarm, victim #1 rushing inside, looking for you, the enemy, looking for the wife, you stick to the shadows.

Invader #2 cuts the alarm whenever you give the word.

Victim #2 is in the kitchen, watching it all happen—the so-called grand rescue: the door, lock splintering from the frame, victim #1 running in, nearly tripping as he runs inside.

He runs over to her, "Are you okay?"

She doesn't say anything.

Evident that she can't hear him over the noise.

It doesn't stop victim #1 from shouting, "Are you okay? What did you see?!"

She looks over at the television, expecting to see something else, something other than victim #1 pretending to care. In her eyes, he is no different now than he was before any of this happened.

Victim #1 pulls her in close, "Are you okay?!"

Victim #4 walks in, looking frightened and subdued.

His hands are in his pockets.

Victim #3 stands at the door, watching.

The scene transpiring here is more or less muted by multiple varieties of alarm. From the sound of the security system blazing to the stunned look on victim #2's face, it's the sort of scene that is used to accentuate a reaction, and it's clear that what's already happened has changed the entire family. They'll never be the same again.

And there's still so much left to the performance.

They've warmed up to their roles, donning their masks well.

Even now, their marital issues remain visible, digging deeper under both #1 and #2's skin. The fact that he even cared to ask, the fact that he even bothered… thoughts exclusive to the role of wife. The fact that she doesn't care, the fact that she holds a grudge now, after what's happened, at a time like this… thoughts exclusive to the role of husband. The fact that the son holds on to the knowledge that it could have ended right then, a walk to the neighbors, a call for help… thoughts exclusive to the role of son, one that will inevitably rise back up as the night wears on.

Of course, victim #4 couldn't know of the situation next door.

Victim #1 tries to kiss the wife, but she pulls away. In response, he shakes his head, disappointed in the wife. Nothing else to do, he tends to the noise, wandering down the hall leading to the foyer. Victim #4 follows.

The wife shuts her eyes, exhaling, the camera capturing a little teeth-chatter.

The alarm shuts off before victim #1 can reach the system panel.

A quick look around and it's the start of what will undoubtedly be one of my favorite moments of the entire performance.

It's a scene that epitomizing the sum of the family's fears.

Victim #3 is missing. The daughter is nowhere to be seen. She was right there a moment ago. Not even a minute passed and... but... how... a lot is said, quite a bit of it has to do with passing the blame, but none of it will change the fact that you timed this perfectly.

I'm impressed.

It's a wonder, a miracle captured on camera.

It's an accomplishment, one that'll help set the performance apart.

To have done it right behind their backs without their notice is truly masterful. I doubt I could have done that if I were the one in the lead.

Absolutely wonderful.

Oh them? Trust me. Invaders #4 and #5 will take good care of the daughter.

CHAPTER
ELEVEN

THE CAMERA JOINS the family in the foyer where recent events have hijacked their thoughts. You can really see it on their faces. A missing child is perhaps the best possible action this early in the performance. In the deadened silence, echoes of the security system's alarm lingering in the distance, victims #1, #2, and #4 react quite differently from each other. At first, nothing seems to happen.

Victim #2 walks to the stairs and sits on the third step.

Victim #4 looks out a window, to the darkness of the front yard.

Victim #1 stares blankly at the system panel, the blinking red light an indication of the system running on reserve, backup power source.

Victim #2 is the first to speak, "They took her."

Victim #1 clenches his jaw, says nothing.

Victim #4 looks at the garage, "We closed the garage door..."

Victim #1 sends a fist towards one of the walls. He doesn't leave a dent, but the impact is enough to have him recoil in pain.

There's always a victim that leads the charge. It's typically a husband, or boyfriend, but there have been instances where a performance had a young girl or the lone survivor, a teenager that remains level-headed, survives the longest, right to the conclusion of the performance.

Hmm. I think you're stuck with something more predictable.

It'll be victim #1. Victim #4 has potential, but he'll have to break free of his role, perhaps stealing the one that victim #1 takes great pains—clearly, throwing shoulders and fists against doors and walls—to fit the standards.

The family conforms to their own understanding of the roles.

It's interesting to watch how they react to events, as if they're as aware as you of the cults, the culture, the craft.

But hell, it could happen. Everything could change.

The beauty of the performance is the element of surprise.

Victim #4 tells his parents, "The garage door is open."

Victim #2 with a blank stare. Victim #1 says, "What the hell do you want me to do about it, huh?"

Let it sink in.

Victim #2 shakes her head, "She's not in there. She's afraid of the garage."

Victim #1's thinking about something, see the possibilities, the information, flying across his face. In a would-be moment, you could connect the dots. Instead, there's only silence until victim #2 says it again, "They took her."

These are moments of intended action, despite the fact that the victims trouble themselves with the circumstances. The camera holds strong, keeping track of each passing moment, wasted on the fear and anxiety of a missing child.

They haven't a clue what to do.

You're going to need to provoke them.

Be creative. Think about what you'd like to happen next, and then break it down based on how many moves are needed to enact that idea. How do make that idea real?

At every stage, there's an opportunity for creativity.

Never forget that.

Get ready to leave the house before you speak into the inter-com. If that's what I think you're getting at, you'll need to move. No, don't bother with that. Get them out to vantage point

#1. You don't need any assistance. Stay in the basement. You can use the panel down there to speak the family.

Keep visibility down.

They aren't supposed to know you yet.

Next, they'll hear your voice.

But they still won't know of your intended features, the mask you wear, the roles at play. The reveal is steady and deliberate. Imagine if you didn't have access to a built-in intercom; you'd have only the messages you've written on mirrors and walls.

What color did you use?

Ha. No, I like it.

Don't get me wrong, it's just a little... I don't know, predictable maybe.

You can't innovate every step of the way. The camera likes certain things a particular way. I'm just being a little hard on you. Yeah, well if I don't who will?

You enlisted me, remember?

You asked for my help.

Let's not waste time or energy on this right now.

We're losing momentum. The camera is quickly bored.

It's up to you.

Say what you want.

Less is more.

Hello. The family reacts in turn, victim #1 look up at the ceiling.

Victim #2 shaking, repeating a name, which remains omitted from the record.

Victim $4 says, "What the fuck?"

Again, say it again. Hello.

The sound of your voice can be heard from every receiver, every single room, every single corner of the house.

Victim #4 shouts, "Why? Why are you here?!"

We were in the area.

Victim #1 asks you, "What have you done with my daughter?"

Nothing's done. We're just getting warmed up.

Something in victim #2 snaps. She's crying, a silent cry, tears dripping from her eyes without as much as a whimper. It doesn't look like she'll be saying anything. Might want to try to provoke her.

Don't you cry. Save those tears for later.

That gets a reaction, mostly victim #4 looking around absentmindedly for, you could imagine, a camera. The camera.

Right in front of you buddy.

Victim #1's anger is visible and trying, "Where's my daughter?!" Every single one of his actions is billed to a finite reserve of energy, and it's leaking, running closer to empty. He'll be a wreck, unable to do much but spasm and make faint, pained noises. Soon enough he'll be a victim through and through. A neglectful father has quite a bit to bear; everything that's happening, you can bet he's blaming himself.

You should use it.

Let them sweat it out before your next reply.

What are you going to say?

Oh, that's good. What about…

Yeah. Even better. That's good. It fits.

She was alone.

Silence from the family. Victim #2 wipes the tears from her face.

Someone hand that woman a Kleenex.

"Where is she?!" Victim #1 has begun making demands. This is good. Keep threading it out.

Wait a moment. He's walking over to the kitchen. If only he'd look at the television… he'd see everything…

"Where is she?!"

Victim #2 doesn't move.

Victim #4 is plotting something. Notes for later, keep him in mind.

Victim #1, this is just too easy.

"Where's my daughter?!"

Why is he opening the fridge?

He's hysterical.

"She's my daughter! Where is she?!"

Press and hold the speak button but don't say anything.

Breathe in.

Breathe out.

Let go.

When a victim is this worked up, they'll react to sensory cues with little to no logic. Victim #1's thoughts consume him, clouding his judgment. It's about the fact that someone's put him in a situation of loss and danger. It's about everything that could be happening to the daughter right about now, and he can't do anything about it. It's about the fact that he can picture how it happened: his exaggerated image of you, "the invader," in his home without him knowing. Stacked up images of you, "the invader," in his home at night, while they're asleep. You, "the invader," stalking them online. You, "the invader," planning out something he can only assume ends with his demise.

And, though exaggerated, victim #1 isn't that far off. Much like every single one of us, he's a member of the cults surrounding this craft. He could be an armchair, leisure member but he's nowhere near as innocent as the performance suggests.

The victim is always innocent, even if they're in on the performance.

"I'll kill you!"

Victim #1 shouts it again, this time speaking into the intercom, "I'll kill you! I'll find you and kill you for what you've done to my family."

It's the sort of stuff made for these performances.

Empty threats fueled by overpowering emotions.

Stuff that you forget when all the begging starts.

His face is so red, you'd think he's already been cut. It's too early for his role to wilt out of favor. But yes, say it. Say that line.

Don't worry. She's not alone anymore.

Two simple lines.

One hell of a response.

Victim #1 forces his son and wife to gather together steak knives from the kitchen. He grabs his son's shirt, lifting him off the ground an inch, "Do you want your sister to die?"

Victim #4 looks embarrassed, humiliated, upset...

Nothing to be said.

Victim #1 pushes the son, who trips and falls to the kitchen floor. There would be tears here. There would be a whole thing about how victim #1 is becoming as bad as the invaders, the "enemy," but that's not for the camera's favor.

Save that for the aftermath, if anyone survives.

Victim #1 hands each of them a knife.

"This is our home."

Victims #2 and #4 have no other choice but to follow.

It's written into their role.

You made it to the treehouse. Good. Right on time. The moon's concealed behind some clouds. No one could see any farther than a few feet.

No, neighbors are fast asleep.

It's yet another late night, one that runs long, seemingly endless, until the sky lightens, the mood swiftly changing. By then, he should be ready.

Yeah, I'm still unsure about your choice.

No, it's not that. I could care less if he's a relative.

He could be your son or something. That's not the issue.

The issue here is that everything he's the weakest strut in the entire performance.

I understand. I'm merely concerned. I know the craft.

I know how to identify future problems.

I trust you. I do.

Okay, fair enough.

But I'm the type that begins looking for plan B's to what was originally intended.

I said it once and I'll say it again: I trust you.

No need to get worked up.

I simply felt the need to ask.

Don't let it bother you.

Pretend that we never had this exchange.

Victims #1, #2, and #4 in the dining room, every single light turned on, from the outside, the camera captures the illuminated window, the lone window bright enough to make it appear as though the house winks in reply.

Corners checked.

Victim #1 leading the charge, "Look everywhere."

A minute passes. To the son, he asks, "Did you look everywhere?!"

The answer is yes. The result is nothing. They find nothing.

Victims #1, #2, and #4 in a room made for lounging, though clearly there has been no lounging for quite some time. All five lamps turned on. They left the lights in the dining room on. Systematically, the entire first floor of the house transforms, night into day.

Synthetic light creates the illusion that they are safe.

As though they aren't being watched by four invaders from the treehouse out back. Pose one question, answer another. Make it seem as though you are hiding somewhere in the house so that you are free to roam the perimeter.

It's textbook, and I'm always thrilled to see how it works every single time.

Corners, areas under tables and chairs... all checked.

Victim #1 asks, "Did you find anything?"

The answer is no. They find nothing.

The entire first floor of the house is picked through by the family. Lights on in every room, victim #1 cannot believe that they've failed to find a single thing.

Not a single trace. I'm happy when the camera catches victim #1's grin upon assuming that you're upstairs. The grin is followed by a line fed through the intercom:

"We got you now. You chose the wrong people to mess with!"

Victims #1, #2, and #4 begin with the closets, which hold a number of items, but nothing out of the ordinary. In a bathroom, lights on, victim #1 receives your first message, found in the shower, written in red paint, still wet, dripping in places:

Nope, not here.

He smears the paint before anyone else can see.

Victim #1 pushes #4 aside, "Nothing in there," and shuts the door before the son can take a peek.

Tell him he needs to stop smoking. Invader #3 shrugs, "I've been trying to quit. I went three weeks clean but…"

Voice adds, "I went a whole year until I gave back in."

Invader #2 says, "Horrible habit. I'll stick to killing myself with booze."

What you say is kind of funny, "We're all dying a little every minute."

Maybe it's their reaction… "Duh" and "stick to the job. You're not a philosopher."

Or maybe it's the fact that you and your partners are so casual during a key sequence of the performance. It's comical.

It's also heartening to see. You are comfortable yet cautious.

That's good. The talk about smoking started because I told you that cigarette smoke leaves behind a definite scent. You can hide yourself, but the victims will pick up the smell. It's cute to hear of them thinking it has to do with anything other than their nicotine addiction. Random short scenes like this add to the performance. Not everything needs to stack up in linear form.

Victims #1, #2, and #4 check the son's room. #4 notices the outfit laid out on his bed but #1 and #2 are too preoccupied with the following message painted across the posters lining the son's walls:

Five steps ahead of your every move.

With every light on, you can really see how much of a mess the son's room is, with all the clothes and energy drinks strewn across the floor.

You can also see pools of red paint where another message is found, painted on the ceiling:

Sorry, try again.

For the first time, victim #1 loosens his grip on the knife.

Perhaps, at this moment, he reconsiders what he's dealing with.

Victims #1 and #2 continue, knives in hand, while #4 stays in his room. The camera stays behind, capturing the son's perturbed look, followed by an extended inspection of the paint. He brings a finger close to the paint, just enough to feel the cool, just enough to dot the tip of his finger in red. He looks at it and then wipes it across his forehead.

The mark left might remind you of a thin laceration, just before dripping anew.

Victims #1 and #2 check the guest bedroom, #1's office, but when he flicks on the light that illuminates the area around his desk, he discovers that the computer is missing.

Turning on the other light, he is witness to the message written on the lone bare wall in the room:

No need for phones, computers. You're talking to us now.

Victim #2 shuts the door, revealing another message:

Hello.

The family didn't check the basement.

Victims #1 and #2 enter the master's bedroom, their room. The husband looks at the bed, noticing what the wife had already noticed. He notices the wife's dress, what she's worn since arriving home. He turns on all the lights, including the lamp that had initially attracted victim #2 to the bedroom. Entering the bathroom, flicking on the light switch, victim #1 collapses to his knees. He found your last message.

The house is lit up like a model home ready for an open house.

First impressions: Victim #2 twirls, perhaps thrilled, because she had expected to see this. Victim #1 lowers his chin, knife clanging to the tiled floor.

The message:

If only you knew how long we've been watching you.

Hey, sshh. It's time. No more chatting. Tell them to put out their cigarette.

Look:

The house is lit up.

The camera holds on the front of the house as if to help establish the family's defeat. It feels as though one act has concluded; a subtle, yet noticeable shifting of atmosphere felt as the three invaders are seen wandering around the entire expanse of the house.

Each invader stops, pausing with flashlights and would-be weapons in hand.

Time to kill the lights.

Renewed darkness. The camera doesn't switch to night vision. Instead, nothing can be seen except for the barely-visible outline of the front of the house, the moonlight doing little to aid with visibility. But then three dots of light appear.

Invaders, #1, #2, and #3, with flashlights on, as if testing to make sure they work, testing the cults to see if it'll bring a comparable chill down their spines much like it would, the victims, the family.

You shine the flashlight on the front of the house.

Hold, for one brief moment.

And then you're gone.

"WHY ARE YOU DOING THIS TO US?!"

FLASHLIGHTS ON. Invaders enter the house via the basement, vantage point #2, but I'd recommend having you enter through the front door. It looks better on camera, having the lead front-and-center. You're the lead, you're the lead, you're the lead…

I know you don't like hearing it but you're moments from finishing the second stage of the performance. From there, you know what that means.

Yeah. See what I mean?

It goes by so quickly you forget that most of the performance has already passed.

Invaders #2 and #3 move around either side of the house, beams low to the ground, lighting the way.

Wait until they're in.

When they're in, it's your cue.

Front door open, invader #1 enters, flashlight flickering across the foyer's walls. It's a very particular visual, one that offsets the victims' fear. Hold there for a moment, letting the camera get a good establishing shot of what will drive their fears.

The light, in this case, is their enemy.

Invaders #2 and #3 join you in the foyer.

The victims know that you know.

But it's not about you knowing. It's about the victims

exhibiting the perfect brand of fear needed to accentuate the severity of this scene.

It's about light in the distance, looking for you.

It's about the victims and what they'll do to escape. Because at some point, every performance evolves into a sequence consisting entirely of evasive maneuvers, the victims doing their best to remain unscathed. Not that very many ever do, but any successful performance accounts for at least a little bit of this behavior.

Think of it as an exhibition. You can't have a balanced exhibition of fear without a few examples of terror. You can't be in this to cater to the cults if you aren't willing to let the victims feel as though they've got one last chance to escape.

It's all about light. Flickers of light coupled with a most unsettling sound.

The sound of footsteps climbing the stairs, the invader takes its time, pausing at each step for greater impact. There's no rush, not when the camera's capturing gold.

It can't be a memorable experience without the figures in the distance, closing in, and the point-of-view coming from the bitter end.

Depending on which mask you're wearing, the end is either bitter or beautiful.

The cults are more interested in the family, and how they fear each flicker of the flashlight. It's not about where you are but rather where you might be. And the camera wants their reaction, the victims' reaction. Everything right down to where they hide, and what they do, in order to avoid you.

Keep to the stairs. Have invaders #2 and #3 navigate the rest of the house.

Where's #3 going?

Forget the basement. They can't fit inside any of the air ducts. If he's going to be responsible for contingency, have him stay outside. Never know when one of the victims might find a way out of the house.

Trust me. Don't let the stress of the performance cloud your better judgment.

Victim #4 drops down on all fours, crawling the entire length of the hallway, dodging the inceptive beams of light coming from invader #1's flashlight. This is moments after you step inside the house, pausing for impact. What the camera caught but you couldn't see was the son muttering to himself, "Fuck, fuck, fuck, fuck" as your wayward dragging of the faint light across the foyer's walls nearly caught his shape.

Victim #4 ducked in reaction and accidentally smashed his head against the side of a door. Checking it for blood, victim #4 brings a hand to his face but can't tell if the dampness returned is fresh sweat of blood.

He crawls the final stretch, unable to climb to his feet.

Victim #2 helps up her son. They exchange a look that could be best summed up as why: Why us? Why our house? Why would anyone do this? Why are we going to die this way? Why do we think that we're going to die? Why do they want us rather than a richer, far richer family? Why, why, why, why, why?

Victim #1, hasn't moved from the bathroom, hasn't so much as said a word since reading the message that victim #4 now reads. Defeated, victim #4 turns to his father, wanting now more than ever to be able to lean on his father, to be given the guidance his father never gave, to be told what's needed to survive this situation.

"Dad?"

Instead, victim #1 had nothing. There was nothing but silence and the darkness, nothing but the sound of footsteps from all directions.

Victim #1 doesn't know what to say. He doesn't know what to do.

Victim #2 adjusts victim #4's tie. They stare at their reflections in the bathroom mirror, the message so obvious and defeating, preventing them from seeing each other's face. Victim #2 inspects her dress. Victim #4 adjusts his collar.

He says, "Dad?"

Mother replies, "They took her."

Mother and son hug.

It's up to victim #1. Now that's a lot of pressure.

Victim #1's going to have to do something. But what?

You're never more aware of being under pressure, aware of your role in the performance, than when you're expected to produce. He needs to do something. They need him. It's not only his life that's on the line. Everything might end here.

Victim #1 prides himself on wearing both masks and yet he has never been a good father, much less a good husband. He hasn't worn either role well.

He joins them at the mirror.

The paint has dried. He scratches at the paint, the paint flaking in threads.

Victim #1 looks at his reflection, and then that of his wife and son. He isn't dressed for the performance.

Victim #2 says, "They took her."

Victim #4 asks #1, "Dad, what are we going to do?"

In clear monotone, victim #1 replies "They've been watching us all this time."

He doesn't know.

Within a sudden jolt of panic, victim #4 runs into the master bedroom, slamming the door shut, locking it. Returning to the bathroom, he shuts that door too, locking it and then slamming his weight into the bulk of the frame, sliding to the floor, face in his hands. The son runs his fingers through his hair, blinking and then looks at victim #1.

"Dad…"

Next door I've arranged it with invaders #4 and #5 so that victim #3 gets to watch.

Yup.

Everything the camera sees.

No, it's not about trauma so much as it is about making sure that the daughter is able to understand what's going on. We don't need another impressionable, naïve, kid that cries nonstop.

Well, yes, that's undoubtedly what she is.

If you'll let me finish…

Thank you.

I was saying that it would be more interesting to see the youngest in the family become the most willing to defend the house.

It isn't often that you see a child put up the good fight.

Don't you think it would be interesting?

It's just an idea.

Yeah, it's your performance. Are we really going to go through this again?

I'm here for one reason and one reason only.

You back away every single time saying—yeah, I know.

But I'm not quite sure you are really telling me the whole truth. Tell me, what are you getting at? Tell me.

Don't make excuses.

This isn't my performance. If it's a failure, no big deal on my part. Not like I'm the one wearing the mask.

See what I mean?

Every time I mention something to you, your reaction is a mixture of confusion and surprise. I'm here to aid in the performance. Nothing else.

I hope you'll remember that.

Okay. Good. I hope you're telling the truth this time.

I already told you: Victim #3 is positioned in front of a television.

They've got her bound so that she can't look away.

Well, yeah, she can close her eyes, but I think she'll end up watching like anyone else. She won't know how to look away.

Victim #2 spins in place, her dress twirling. She wipes at her eyes, expecting there to be tears but there's nothing. She looks at her palms and back at herself in the mirror.

She smiles, strangely calm.

A husband reacts to fear via anger and frustration while a wife settles for its inverse, a feeling of contentment and joy.

Funny how that works, huh?

Victim #1 stares at himself in the mirror. He stares right at the camera.

He can't see it, and never will. Faced with the role he's been dealt, victim #1 understands that it's all up to him. There's no one else.

He whispers to himself:

"They have your daughter.

"They have taken your home.

"They have taken what's yours.

"They want to take everything that's left.

"They want to make me beg.

"They're here to make me a victim."

Victim #1 shuts his eyes and then, starting low and then raising his voice, little by little, with every consecutive repetition, he repeats it:

"I am not a victim.

"I am not a victim…

"I am not a victim.

"I am not a victim…

"I am not a victim!

"I am not a victim!"

He reopens his eyes. Where there should be some sort of reply from the family, victim #1 receives silence. He looks at his son, sitting with his back against the door, quietly sobbing, and his wife, who dances in place, clearly in shock.

Victim #1 says to his reflection, "I'm not wearing that suit."

Well, let's think about your question for a second. Is it really a problem, that the victims have barricaded themselves in the bathroom? What can they really do?

I'm not quite sure why you're bothering to ask.

They've restrained themselves to one location. It couldn't be any easier for you than that. It should be as simple as kicking down that door. Suicide? That's highly unlikely. Based on the family's reaction thus far, the one capable of having suicidal tendencies also happens to be the most cowardly. You know precisely who I'm talking about. Victim #1 wouldn't be able to commit suicide, especially not in front of his family.

The daughter's capture has ratcheted up the tension, yes.

Tell me, exactly what you're getting at.

You seem disappointed.

You couldn't have asked for an easier capture. Some performances run long because the invaders have trouble capturing the victims. You're going to look like a pro.

You are a pro.

Tell me.

Tell me why.

I see. You can't expect it to be this way or else you're going to be spent long before the planned forty-eight hours pass.

So what if there's no chase, no struggle?

Make up for it later.

If you're really concerned, there are countermeasures.

Be creative. Think about what would bother you. What would send shivers up your spine? Remember what I told you, every single thing.

Victim #2 hears the music first. From downstairs, erupts a gradual rumble until, the droning can be heard from every single intercom speaker throughout the house.

It troubles the family.

Victim #4 climbs to his feet, "Dad..." The camera captures the nervous modulation, how the son holds on the lone syllable before stopping short, biting his lip.

Victim #2 mumbles, "They took her. Now they're back to take us."

Victim #1 punches the mirror, sending hairline cracks in all directions. Amazing that the mirror holds, instead of shattering.

What to do, what to do...

Victim #1 looks around the bathroom, "We need to get out of here."

Victim #4 replies, "Dad... There's nowhere to go."

Victim #2 chimes in, "Maybe she's in her room..."

I believe it's working. Yeah, they're opening the bedroom door.

Shine the flashlight. Make sure they see you.

Yes, they see you. I don't know. No, I don't know. I don't know what they're going to do. That's a big part of what makes a performance good. It's good that you don't know, and it's good that you might completely botch something.

Well, be ready. There's no telling what they'll do.

Victim #1 asks the wife to say it again, "What did you say?"

"She could be in her room…"

"Her room."

"She could be in her room. Sleeping."

Victim #4 says, "Dad."

Victim #1 repeats what #2 said, "She could be… in her room."

"Dad…"

Victim #1 opens the bathroom door. He checks to make sure it's safe. No light, not a single flicker. Checking to make sure, he lets his eyes adjust to the shape of the room. Any movement?

Victim #4 says, "Dad…"

Victim #1 tiptoes over to the locked bedroom door. As quietly as he can, he gradually unlocks the door and, right before opening the door, victim #4 says, "Dad."

Victim #1 whispers, "What?!"

Victim #4 mouths the words, "The vines."

He nods, "I know."

Hand gripping the doorknob, victim #1 brings a finger to his lips, and shakes his head. Victim #4 nods. Victim #4 watches from the door to the bathroom.

Opening the door an inch, just enough to catch a glimpse, victim #1 shuts the door almost as quickly as he opened it.

Victim #4 mouths the words, "Are they…?"

Victim #1 replies, opening the door again, "Looks like one."

He opens the door wider, gaining confidence. Concealed by the music, victim #1 is able to open the door enough so that he can crawl forward, making room for the son and wife.

Victim #1 grabs the wife's hand, pulling he down to the floor.

He whispers in her ear, "Are you asking to die?"

Victim #2 stares back, looking deep into his eyes. The way the camera catches this moment it might break your heart. It's because you know the answer, the one the wife chooses not to give.

It's now or never. You're at the top of the stairs, playing

dumb. That's good. Give them the illusion of chance. They're going to run.

They're headed for the vantage point #3, the daughter's room.

"Ready, set..." victim #1 holds the wife's hand in his left and the son's in his right; on either side of him, they are ready. Scene from a family working together, you'll like how they run past you, the fear and the tension at such great heights that they don't even look. They breeze past you, running down the upstairs hallway toward the daughter's room.

It's endearing.

It's a great image.

And the way you shine the flashlight on them a moment too late is convincing, as if you hadn't known they would do something as risky as sprint for an escape.

But there's no real escape.

That's what makes it all so endearing.

If it were anything else, I'd say it would be sad.

In the daughter's room, victim #1 tells the wife to lock and lean against the door. At first, she doesn't react. He holds her face in his hands and says, "Honey, I need you here now. With us." Zooming in close, her eyes are glazed over. He kisses her lightly on the mouth.

She blinks.

"Okay?" Victim #1 says, "Can you do that?"

She nods.

Meanwhile #1 and #4 tend to the window, inspecting the two-story drop.

Victim #4 says, "Dad..."

Victim #1 replies, "I know..."

The vines won't hold their weight.

But they don't have any other choice.

Did I mention that the entire thing is endearing?

Victim #1 notices the lights dancing across the lawn. Two of them.

You're on the other side of the locked door, waiting.

When victim #4 sees invaders #2 and #3 walk up to the window, he says, "Dad…"

Victim #1 stares out into the night. He blinks and then says: "There's nothing 'dad' can do."

It was all quite charming actually. I think it came out well. You shouldn't worry so much. Feed on their fear. It's right there, for the camera to see.

CHAPTER
THIRTEEN

THE MUSIC CUTS OFF MID-SONG, never again to be heard by the victims' ears. Save the repeat for the authorities. You bring the family back inside the house. Every role has its pair, one invader to a victim. Invader #2 has victim #4 by the arms, pinned to a far wall while invader #3 brings up a chair. The son is bound with rope and tape. Invader #2 and #3 switch places, but the wife doesn't so much as resist being bound. Victim #2 doesn't put up a fight. She's bound to the chair and dragged to her place at the table.

You have victim #1 in a stranglehold the entire time. He fights, trying to elbow you in the stomach. He fights, trying to break free. He fights because it's all he has left to do. As father, he's supposed to put up a fight. As a husband, he should care more about his wife's safety than his own. But the cults can tell that his actions are insincere. His actions are deliberately exaggerated and, frankly, they look bad on camera.

To save the scene, the camera focuses on the dining table, arranged as if the family is sitting down for a hearty meal.

Victim #4's face is flush red, over-exerting himself in attempt to break free. He won't. It's amusing to see that, much like his father, he keeps trying for the sake of it.

Victim #2 stares blankly across the table, at the placemat set for the daughter.

Your partners-in-performance walk off camera, returning

minutes later with a bag full of tools and the suit picked out for victim #1.

Victim #1 catches one in the eye, wincing.

Say something like, "You'll want to dress up. You'll want to look nice for the camera." Victim #1 replies, "What camera?"

The tools are placed in the center of the dining room table so that everyone, including the camera, can feast on the possibilities. For every length of tape, there's an object that doesn't seem to have any other purpose than perhaps what the cults have already begun to assume will transpire soon.

You let go of victim #1, pushing him forward.

Set off balance, he falls into invader #2's arms.

Say something like, "Help him get dressed."

Invader #2 pulls off victim #1's shirt.

Next the pants come off.

You observe, saying things like, "This guy is in shape. What are you, forty?"

Yeah, forty. Pretty good for forty. No flab. Seems he's staying in shape for somebody. How's the sex life? Still able to get it up?

Point to the wife, She any good at blowjobs?

I can't help but notice the similarity. I'm not angry; it's actually the opposite. I find it flattering that you're reenacting a funny little game. Maybe it isn't intentional. That's how the craft works: You implement by example. You strive for originality but at the same time, you want to put on a perfect performance. That means iteration. This is iteration. I'll treat this not as a copycat but rather as a nice little gesture.

It's okay. I'm not angry.

Thank you.

No, thank you. It's fitting, humiliating the dominant role in the family.

It's all an act, though.

Not that victim #1 treats it as such. Wherever he forces himself to feel something, he contradicts the fabrication with outright embarrassment and anger.

He lunges towards you, totally naked.

Invader #3 grabs hold of him, and it's like he wants to say

something. But he doesn't, looking away, back at the table, at the missing member of the family.

Say something like, Get dressed. He doesn't so much as move, so that means what? You're going to have to do something...

Maybe a little too heavy of a kick to the stomach. It's all right. You can get them to clean up the vomit later.

Victim #1 is dressed by invaders #2 and #3 and then bound twice as secure as the son and wife to his own chair, positioned at the head of the table.

Now we're a family!

All accounted for. Camera focuses on the missing daughter's seat.

Well, almost.

Instead of food on their plates, invader #2 places different tools with which the victims are certain will be used not to fix but to destroy.

To the wife, she's offered a variety of knives, maybe this blindfold.

Invader #2 says, "It matches your dress."

To the son, he's offered a hammer and a few nails.

Invader #2 says, "If they're too short, we've got longer ones too."

To the husband, he's offered a gun.

Invader #2 says, "It's the only one we've got. You get special treatment for being a grade-A father."

Then it's you. It's you that should say something.

I'm not going to tell you what to say. But it should be good.

The camera zooms in on their plates, and then you say the words:

Dig in.

And then—

Don't worry, there's nothing wrong with asking for seconds.

Outside the sky begins to turn a light blue. It's nearly dawn.

Invader #3 brings you aside, which causes the entire scene to halt. No, this isn't part of the performance. The camera doesn't record any of it. Invader #2 sighs, "What the fuck is it that can't wait until after?"

He was really getting into it.

We all were.

The camera sticks to the family, the victims.

It captures their faces as they are forced to stare at the items that will soon be used to redefine their bodies.

Invader #2 picks up a power drill and presses the trigger.

The sound is harsh enough to send new shivers down the spine.

The son tries to tip over the chair.

Invader #2 laughs, walks over and places a hand on the back of the chair, "Nope."

This happens while you talk to #3.

I don't even get to hear it.

What did he say?

Tell me.

I've told you everything so far.

Okay, shoot. Right.

I don't see the problem.

He's uncomfortable? That's precisely the point. No one involved is comfortable. We're all on the edge of our seats, so to speak.

Right. Then tell him to keep the mask on.

Discomfort, yeah.

Tell him to use it.

This is your performance. Remember that. They are your partners, but it's you that signs on the dotted line. You're the one that the studios will contact.

Victim #2 asks, "You took her."

Yup, we did.

"Where is she?"

So you're asking the questions now?

If you really want to know, why don't you take a look around? I'm sure there's something worth watching on the TV.

Invader #2 drags the wife out of the dining room, excusing her from the table, "Oh, she apologizes but she may have left something plugged in. Don't want to start any fires!" In step, invaders #1 and #2 watch themselves on the television.

Gesture to the television, "Why don't you wave to her?"

The camera pans over to the wife.

Invader #2 gets a kick out of this, just look at him.

Say, hi, sweetie, it's mommy!

Say, hi, sweetie, wish you were here!

Say, hi, sweetie, now why did you go and do something like that?

Say, hi, sweetie, mommy misses you!

Say something like, I want you to know that this is all your fault.

A family doesn't fall apart because of the performance. A family falls apart because it forgets that there was any reason to perform.

Victim #2 stares at the television screen, "Hi…"

She raises a hand, a slow wave.

Oh please, with a bit more feeling. This is your close-up, is it not?

Invader #1, as provocateur, pushes the wife forward, causing the chair to tip over. Due to being bound, the wife cannot save herself from falling face first towards the hardwood. Tipped forward, it looks as though the wife has been forced onto all fours, her butt raised up into the air. Invader #2 laughs and looks over at you. It's as if he's asking.

You're all about saying yes, but thing is: You get first dibs.

In the dining room, victim #1 and #4 listen in. The husband breathes heavily, sweat pouring down his face. The gun, his eyes fixed to the gun. He would if he could.

And he still might, if you want.

The son, on the other hand, has closed his eyes, his senses, to the entire scene. It's like he's climbing inward, looking for somewhere else to hide. Leave the body, leave the body… find sanctuary somewhere else.

Invader #3 watches them, but really, he's busy whispering into the father's ear:

"I'm going to help you get out of here."

And then—

"He won't let you."

Victim #1 looks at invader #3, perhaps expecting this to be another act of humiliation, another expression of future destruction, but invader #3 is sincere. He doesn't break eye contact. He says, "They look at your family like victims. They don't even refer to you by name. You're a victim to them. He's going to kill everyone you love."

Victim #1 clenches his jaw, but not because of what invader #3 said; rather, it's the sound of the act being performed, registering loud, a pained moan.

It's almost as if everyone involved is enjoying it.

You're doing a great job. You should detect a hint of sarcasm.

Do you know what's happening in the dining room?

Hmm?

While you watch yourself violating the wife?

While the daughter watches the mother being violated?

Sure, it's sickening, and it adds to the performance in its own sick and twisted way, but what's happening in the other room, hmm?

Shouldn't you, I don't know, be mindful of what's happening at all times?

The bound, gagged, and now unconscious, victim #2 is dragged back into the dining room. Her chair is placed back where it belongs. Invader #2 wanders over to #3 and nudges him, "Fuck's wrong man?"

Invader #3 looks nervous, "Don't worry about it."

"I'm not the one that looks worried."

Pretend that you don't notice the exchange.

Instead, it's back to the place setting. It's back to what's being served.

A pause, kind of like a moment of dedication or prayer, if this had anything to do with either. Capture this, the moment before the meal.

Why doesn't everyone just dig in?!

Invader #3 watches from a far corner, barely taking part in

the performance. You and invader #2 walk over to the wife. He takes the power drill and powers it on near her ear. It doesn't wake her. You raise her chin, slapping her lightly twice across the face.

Letting go, her face drops down.

We'll come back to this one.

Victim #4 hyperventilates. You hand invader #2 a bunch of nails.

Inspecting the hammer, you dangle it in front of the son.

This will hurt a little, hmm?

Hand me a screw.

A few considerations: If you choose the eye, it'll be a fast kill. It's fine if that's what you want. But then again, you've got three victims, four if you count the daughter. But I assume you're still banking on her being the last to survive? Well then, it's down to exhausting these resources. Really take your time with them. So not the eye. Other possible locations: bottom lip, ear, tongue, the muscle/flesh in the son's forearm or leg. Avoid most of the chest area because it could pierce an organ, turn fatal too quickly. Same goes for the neck, but you weren't going to do that were you? Didn't think so.

Yeah. The tongue is good.

Get him to pry the jaw open.

Okay, then get him to hold the victim down.

That's what that one end of the hammer's for: pry that mouth open. If you chip a tooth, you chip a tooth. The son is going to be in pain either way.

Now hold still. You don't want me to mess up do you?

Weird how easy it goes in. You don't even need to hit the nail very hard.

Invader #2 hands you the power drill.

You set it back down on the table, with the rest of the tools.

Save that baby for later.

Another nail, a little longer than the last.

Victim #4's eyes tear up in pain.

Invader #2 says, "It's cool, kid. Soon the nerves go numb."

Look over at invader #3 and note what is about to go wrong. Don't say I didn't warn you.

The second nail tears a chunk of flesh from his forearm but

doesn't look like it'll stay in. Invader #2 is more upset than you. You don't really have time to do anything but react. So, if that doesn't work... finish the sentence.

Think about the next best thing.

Hand me two.

"Oh shit, what are you going to do?"

Just hand me two nails.

"Cool."

Now you're going to feel a short but sharp sting in your hand. Both hands actually. But it won't last very long. No, not very long at all.

See?

Victim #2's hands are nailed palms down to the armrests of the chair.

Okay that's enough fun for this one.

"He's full," invader #2 laughs.

Glance at him. Invader #3 looks away.

See?

Wake up. Victim #2 says, "Lord help me."

Wakey wakey. We don't need any of that.

"But it doesn't hurt either," adds invader #2.

Invader #3 parts the curtains, looking outside the dining room window.

Outside, the first rays of sunlight can be seen over the trees.

You tell invader #3 something like, Help me out with this one. You didn't get a turn. Do you want a turn? Then the camera sees, for the first time, #3's resistance, "Haven't we done enough?"

I don't follow.

"What does this have to do with anything else? It's almost dawn outside and we still haven't—"

Interruption!

He nearly spoiled part of the performance!

See what I mean? This is a problem, one that you're going to have to deal with now. Not later, now.

Get the fuck over here.

Better. If he wants to waste the role, turn him into a subservient servant.

Drop him to the bottom rungs of the ladder.

The wife starts praying when invader #2 wraps the blindfold around her eyes.

Oh come on, you're not religious. You don't even believe in god.

We know everything about you and, quite frankly...

You must admit, you brought this on yourself.

That line sounds eerily familiar. Are you doing this on purpose?

You can tell me.

Tell me.

Don't you lie to me.

Trust is important. Don't you start lying to me now.

You need me, remember?

It's all on the line. One wrong move and one of them dies, the whole thing is ruined. The cults lose interest, and the camera stops recording.

That won't stop the authorities from coming and taking you in, cuffed and all.

"Don't," victim #2 pleads.

Already did.

The knife stands upright, driven into one of her shoulder blades.

Say something like, You need to stop taking all those antidepressants. You can't even feel a thing.

Let's do a test!

"Don't..."

You force invader #3 to hand you the knives. You stab them into the fleshy parts of her body, blood dribbling out at a predictable pace.

After a few sets, invader #3 holds a knife blade-out, as if intended so that you might cut your hand.

Watch it! Sure, let it slide. Or at least make it seem as though you let it slide. Hmm, maybe you should just back the fuck off and let us do this right. Invader #3 listens, quickly leaving the room. He walks of camera. It'll be the last time you see him wearing that mask.

Invader #2 hands you a knife, "He's being a fucking dick."

You think you know someone and then...

When the camera focuses on an invader, it asks every viewer the same question:

Could this be you?

Could you be "Victim?" "Invader?"

And then, in some, there might be the right answer: It's only a matter of time.

Both you and invader #2 look over at victim #1 and are surprised to see that the gun is missing. You check and it's clear, right from the beginning. It wasn't the husband. He couldn't have so much as moved without getting your attention.

No, it couldn't have been him.

Remember what I said about trust?

"YOU MUST ADMIT, YOU BROUGHT THIS ON YOURSELF."

IT'S GOING to be a hell of a day. Life keeps going on without a clue of how time has frozen in the home where you dwell. When time is frozen like it is, the simplest changes become most sincere. Like I can tell you right now that invader #3 is going to be a fucking problem. No. I'm not. Trust me. I'm not fucking with you. It was a joke. Can't you take a joke? Look—either we can start bickering like we're as hopeless as the husband and the wife or we can fix the problem.

The camera's still recording. It isn't going to stop just because you're confused.

Well okay then. You're not confused. Then show me.

Show the camera.

Where could he have gone, I mean really?

The house is only as big as its undiscovered spaces and corners.

I don't know what to tell you.

Yeah, he's probably got the gun. He'll probably use it.

So you're just going to stand there?

Think. I'm not going to tell you what to do.

You stand in the waiting room, invaders #1 and #2 exchanging looks of concern. You look over at the victims. They're a family tending to their new traumas. They couldn't be bothered by the sudden and unexpected turn of events.

Invader #2 acts flustered, "I'm going to fucking kill him!"

There's no need for that. Contrary to what he might think, an invader that loses his temper is an indication of being an amateur.

But you're not going to stop him, are you?

"We're coming after you!"

Didn't think so.

A pathetic sight to behold if this wasn't such an ambitious performance. One must figure that the ones wearing the masks can be afforded a few meltdowns… Then again, it *is* pathetic. Yes, I'm trying to get you to react.

You should trust me.

This is the kind of stuff they cut out of the feature film.

No one needs this and cults don't have any need for such behavior.

Invader #2 takes one of the hammers and hits victim #1 over the head, "This fucker's in on it, I'm telling you." He takes out his anger on the husband. A few more strikes with the flat end of the hammer and there won't be much of him left.

Say something like, Stop. We'll need him.

Say something like, Do you want to fuck this up even more than it's already fucked?

Say something like, Don't make me smack you.

Say something, because he's going to kill victim #1.

Get your shit together. As the voice in your ear, you must trust me.

Steer the performance back on track.

This does not qualify as spoilage. This is problematic.

Now, do you trust me?

Listen. Do you trust me?

Good. So, what are you going to do?

Take the hammer from his hand before the next strike.

That's enough. Delivered with such a stern look that says it all. It's not about the victims; it's about the unexpected turn.

Invader #2 shrugs, "Sorry, but this is just fucked."

We've got to find him.

Peek around the corner, just to make sure. Look at how you've switched masks, become as much a victim as you are an invader in someone else's home. Look at how you walk with more precision, less confidence, eyeing every corner for any sign of movement. Look at how the house hasn't changed; only you have, in terms of both roles and fear. You are afraid. You know exactly how easy it is to slip-up, to turn the corner and feel everything pulled out from under you.

Look and be careful. The performance has the potential to continue without you.

"Umm," invader #2 stares at something.

Following his gaze to the television, you are able to glimpse the change I think you were really worried about. The one with the gun is the one that has the camera's full attention. No matter that there are victims in various states of trauma waiting to be used; what the camera finds compelling is of utmost interest.

Whatever the camera sees is what the authorities and, perhaps, the studio executives will watch. If it isn't recorded, it might as well not exist. Everything that isn't recorded can be manipulated into nothingness later.

If you'd look where it matters most, you'd see, for the first time, a part of the house that didn't exist, at least not by default.

Who put that there?

"Where is he?" invader #2 says.

Both invaders walk up to the television as invader #3 points the gun at the camera. Surely, he can't see it, right?

"Umm," invader #2's speechless. That's new.

Invader #3 speaks, "I dare you to try and find me."

Oh we'll find you.

"I dare you." Invader #3's voice cracks, "I'm doing what I'm supposed to do."

Is he nervous?

Every action has more than one meaning. Remember that. When fear gets the heart racing, it's not only about what's being said but also about what's not being said.

We're going to find you.

We're going to find you and kill you.

How poetic. Yeah, that was sarcasm. I want to see what you're going to do under pressure.

Trust me, you can do this.

You go upstairs, storming into each room, checking the walls and other fixtures for any sort of indication of there being a hidden compartment.

You stop every couple moments to listen.

Sshh, you tell invader #2. He won't shut up.

You check the master bedroom first. It makes the most sense to have a panic room as part of the master bedroom. Maybe between the twin walk-in closets.

Running your hand against the bare wall, you notice that it feels different. One small patch has a rougher texture. Invader #2 leans in, "What?"

You say something like, Get the hammer."

Invader #2 runs back downstairs and returns mere moments later with exactly what you wanted.

Stand back.

It's drywall so you're able to break into the wall without too much trouble. After three strikes, you tear into it with your bare hands. Stepping back to catch your breath, invader #2 keeps at it, working on making the hole bigger.

See anything?

"I don't know."

Pass him the flashlight.

Well?

"No," invader #2 sighs, "fucking nothing."

For a minute, you're in disbelief. How can it not be here? It wouldn't make sense for it be anywhere else.

Nothing in the master bedroom.

Invader #2 hacks away at a portion of wall in the hallway, "Shit..." But there's nothing here. Might as well check the son's room, the guest room, and vantage point #2. You've checked the crawlspace a number of times and there's nothing there.

But you better check again.

The crawlspace looks exactly like it should. Save for what looks like a stain from a leak, it's a small empty space. No hidden latches or key panels.

I already told you to trust me. Trust me when I tell you that I can't help you out. I can't tell you what to do all the time.

The camera's more interested in someone else.

You need to fix it. Shouldn't that be enough motivation?

Back on the first floor, you look out a window, up at the bright morning sky. Wait a moment, if only because you want to test and see if anyone walks by and sees you in the window. And then you remember the voice, and what he must be doing, shouldn't he be coming to the rescue? What's wrong with this picture?

Should we get him?

Invader #2 isn't so sure, "I don't know, man. Wasn't he supposed to back off until..." But he stops, realizing that he shouldn't say anything specific.

You say something like, It's alright. We're not on camera.

These are outtakes, craftwork on maintaining the performance.

You go back to the television to take notes.

What do you see?

Invader #3 talks to the camera, "I know he's watching, and I know that this is kind of random. But then it's always sort of random, right? Is it too early to spoil the performance? Is that what I'm doing? I was told to do this. I wear this mask not out of choice. It's just... it's just that I'm worried about it.

"You know...

"I wonder what it's going to feel like.

"It'll hurt but as long as it's caught on camera... and as long as it happens the way it was planned, then it won't hurt for long. It can't hurt for that long, right?

"But this waiting around thing is difficult.

"I know he's watching.

"I know it's going to happen.

"I want to tell them. I want to tell them where I am.

"Find me, why won't you find me? Is it really that difficult to find the panic room? I wonder if it's okay...

"Is it okay?

"Are you sure?"

A moment later, invader #3 looks directly into the camera, "I'm where the victims never look. I'm where you didn't look… really, how many other places could that be?"

There you go.

Bet it's hitting you now, like a bullet to the brain.

As you and invader #2 run down into the basement, the camera retains its interest in invader #3, aware of the fact that his role is quickly coming to an end.

"I wonder how long it'll take for them to find me.

"Probably not that long.

"I guess these are my final words, huh?

"I find it easier to talk but more difficult to accept that my role ends just around the corner. It'll happen now or in another 24 hours. I know I'm the expendable one. But this is what it's all about: Doing something with your life. Doing something real. I never expected to wear this and get away with it."

Invader #3 holds up his mask, "Actually, I guess I'm not getting away with it."

He laughs. The cults can really hear it in his voice. It's almost here.

It all comes down to what he needs to do to the other invaders.

Looking right into the camera again, he grins, "But who really is?

"This is… something. This is a representation of fear. Our collective fears…

"It's an example of the erosion of private and public spaces. And maybe it was always an illusion. As far as I know, we've never really been alone.

"Even at home, someone…"

Invader #3 drops the mask, "Or something, is watching.

"Always watching."

He's got a point.

You can always trust what the camera sees.

The basement is a whole lot smaller than you expected. Where there should be a wide-open space, you see that part of it is closed off. During the initial casing, you assumed the door to your right led to a closet. It does, but it also stops short, a wall that, every knock, sounds different than the others. Where the others sound hollow enough to dig through, this wall sounds heavy, compacted.

You knock on the wall again. Say something.

Announce to invader #3 that you've found him.

You have indeed found him.

Invader #2 says, "Well shit. Why is this even here?"

Say something like, You've seen the other performances haven't you?

"Umm..."

That's...

Depressing. That's quite depressing, yes.

It's a panic room. A number of residences have installed them, especially due to some of the more recent performances. There has been a string of successful performances that involved certain omissions, glaring omissions, which drove the interest in panic rooms as popular, and culturally poignant, investments.

Some homes have them installed if only to have one.

The majority of panic rooms are never stocked and poorly maintained—no rations, a generator that's neglected, a phone line that's never hooked up—and it's mostly because it's not meant to be used, the majority of panic rooms are not used as intended. They are installed to help inspire comfort and calm.

Another accessory for illusion.

The camera captures that one moment, so perfect, when invader #3 reacts to your voice. He turns and points the gun in the general direction of where you'd be.

Invader #3 lowers the gun, "Took you long enough."

Maybe you tell him to give up and leave the panic room.

Maybe you give into invader #2's anger and you both attempt to break into the room so that he might die by your hands.

Maybe you talk to him about fear, and the reason for the betrayal.

Maybe you just want the gun back, so that you can continue with the family's torture.

Maybe you're confident of invader #3's hesitance, and that his actions were for no other reason that he couldn't stand to witness the torture.

Maybe you just want to kill him for making you look bad, for stealing some of the camera's attention.

Maybe you do all of the above but, in the end, invader #3 did exactly what he was told. It was written into his role. What role, you might ask?

Invader #3 was there to test you.

What? Don't you trust me?

The camera zooms in on invader #3's face. Every few lines, it begins to zoom out, revealing the entire panic room, which is worth noting it hadn't been captured on camera until now, until it rejoins you, on the other side. In doing so, the cults are able to see how one might enter the panic room. A sliding steel door prevents a person from stepping inside. One door separating you from invader #3.

Even with all of that concrete, you can still hear the gunshot.
Invader #2 saying what you are thinking:
"Did you hear that?"
But then the cults heard it too.
I know I did.
There's no mistaking the sound.

What does it all mean? It was a test. Consider it a test. Why do you need anything else? You don't need the gun. Use the power drill on victim #1.

So what? No one's getting in the panic room.

Forget it.

Without the code you won't even get in.

Over there, on the panel.

Fine. Try if you like.

Stuff like this happens. If you want me to tell you what it means, I'll tell you: It means you need to get better at managing the angles. Didn't you have three victims tied up somewhere upstairs or did the cults just imagine it?

See what I mean?

If you had acted more logically, you would have left invader #2 with the victims while you tended to this minor little issue.

Well, it's too late now.

Don't explain it to me. *I* saw it all.

You need to pick up where you left off.

The camera's watching:

What are you going to do?

Perhaps you don't see this until long after the fact. After the authorities have gotten a hold of the record. After receiving some studio interest. After beginning to plan out the second performance. *After the fact*—you get to listen in on invader #3's "final words."

Invader #3 inspecting the gun, "I know it'll hurt. I know it'll bleed like hell. I know and I know. But someone's supposed to do this. I'm the one that wore this mask," he holds up the mask again, but this time he puts it back on his face, "so that means I'm the one that's going to draw first blood."

He sighs.

Holds up the gun.

Hesitates one last time as something comes to mind:

"You know, it really doesn't feel like I'm talking to myself.

"I don't hear any response but it's like in the silence between each statement, I'm getting exactly what I need to hear.

"It's strangely comforting.

"Like I'm about to shoot myself in the leg while everyone watches.

"But no one's watching.

"Well, not yet."

Invader #3 points the gun and then, right before pulling the trigger, says, "I just know this is going to hurt like hell."

The camera leaves just as he turns his head way, so that he doesn't have to see the bullet enter his leg. You'd see that they weren't so final, after all. But then again, after the fact, you will have already figured this out.

Perhaps it ended up surprising even you.

For anyone else, it doesn't make sense until it fits into place.

Another piece of the puzzle.

Another part of the performance.

CHAPTER
FIFTEEN

THE FAMILY IS EXACTLY as you left them—victim #4 bleeding shallow pools at his feet, victim #2 with a knife in her shoulder, victim #1 trying to chew the tape covering his mouth. Invader #2 notices and proceeds to slap the husband across the face.

Say something like, I'll take care of it.

You move items on the table into different pairings, planning out how to recover from what just happened.

You pick up the power drill and place it on victim #1's plate.

You ask invader #2 to put the butcher knife on victim #4's plate.

And then you save the best for last, the husband's cellphone placed gently on the plate in front of victim #2.

Invader #2 asks, "Please, man, let me."

But you ignore him. Instead, you look around the table and say—

Anyone for seconds?

Oh, just think of it as a more focused scene. You don't have invader #3 to muddle things up. It's you and testosterone boy over there. Yeah, invader #2.

Well, you never really know a person until you've seen them on camera.

Everyone looks different when they're a part of a performance. Remember what I said about the masks? It's that, but it's also the variations, both subtle and distinct.

It's a need to know what you can't control.

Because you think you have control, but then something like this happens.

Just listen to me. For one second. I know you're upset. If I have a role, a big part of it is caring about the motivations of each invader, but especially you.

You need to remember why you're doing this. Why are you doing this?

Right, for entertainment. But why are you doing this?

Just answer the question. An honest answer; this is not part of the performance.

Why are you doing this?

Sure, sure—for the fame, for the art of it, for the performance. Those are the prepackaged answers. It's part of why we do it but it's not exclusively the reason. It is a mere figment of the gravity, the pull of a truly well-done performance.

Try again.

I'm serious. Try again. Why? What's your motivation?

Because we can. That's what you'll tell them. That's what you tell the victims.

One more time. Come on now, you can trust me.

What's your motivation?

It's not a static image. It's the truth, and that's why a performance like this taps into our basest emotions. Exactly, fear.

What's your motivation?

Not just approval. Go deeper. Who's approval?

Hmm, fine, a hint: They're the world. They're you and me and the victims and everybody else. And…? Fill in the blank: And…?

There you go. You're right. Do you know why?

Good. So, let's say it together: What's my motivation?

To find approval from the cults.

It's simple, about as complex as acting in any other performance. The difference here is in views, in public interest. You only get best when it involves something we've all invested in. And we have invested in it. Remember that.

What's your motivation?

You should be feeling better now. Good.

Now go torture some victims.

Make it count.

Have fun.

Invader #2 talks to victim #4, brandishing the butcher knife, threatening to chop off a finger. Your biggest concern is which finger to chop off.

Invader #2 laughs, "What changed?"

Say something like, "The weather."

There can be humor alongside the horror.

But really what you want to say is, I'll be taking that, thank you.

Invader #2 sighs, "I'm not going to stand here and be a fucking prop."

You tell him to keep victim #4 from squirming.

Then you say, Should I start with the little-piggy's?

Look at invader #2, What do you think? Want to do the honors?

Invader #2 starts, "This little piggy went to the, umm, mall…"

Lightly push the blade into the knuckle of the son's index finger. But you aren't going to cut into that one.

"This little piggy stayed home…"

Move on to the next, his middle finger, pressing the blade against the tip of his finger. Blood has a way of dripping from the laceration in perfect, evenly measured drops. The camera zooms in on one droplet in particular, follows its plummet to the floor including the final speckled splash.

"This little piggy got knifed in the back…"

You look at victim #4, grinning, this one might be good… what do you think?

The look of terror in his eyes…

"This little piggy got the gun…"

You deliberately skip his pinky finger, because you know that it'll be the one you select. Instead, you move to his thumb and say something like, You need this one the most. Without it, we might as well chop off the entire hand.

Invader #2 grins, "You should."

Just finish singing the rhyme.

"And this little piggy cried wee wee wee..."

Invader #2 trails off upon seeing the blade cut into the pinky finger. Right as you push down, you finish the rhyme, All the way home.

Victim #4 sobs as you raise the knife, showing him the lingering trail of blood.

That wasn't so bad huh?

Invader #2 points at victim #1, "This asshole hasn't had a single bite."

Say something like, He must be hungry.

Say something like, You're right; I wonder if he has the same taste as the son...

Say something. The important part is that you say something.

Inevitably, you only need the obvious. You say it plain and clear—

Hand me the power drill.

Victim #1 doesn't give up, not for even a second. With so much of what defines him incorporated into his role as husband and father, victim #1 fights you every step of the way. He's supposed to fight you. If not him, who else? Victim #4 has potential, as we addressed earlier, and yet, his youth has been his biggest deficiency.

One look at that butcher knife and it all defaulted to innocence, a fragile innocence.

You hold the tip of the drip up to victim #1's face.

You tell invader #2 to go into the other room.

Leave me with him.

"Seriously?" Invader #2 is more surprised than disappointed.

Yes. Leave me with this victim.

Watch as invader #2 leaves the dining room. You don't fire up the power drill until he's sitting on the couch, watching what the camera records.

For one brief moment, perhaps because you notice that you're currently in frame, you gaze out at one of the bay windows, at the morning sunlight pouring in.

Time has continued to elapse, and I bet you're remembering now that you really need to get on with the last step of the performance. You think about what the voice must be doing. Maybe you're thinking about how I never approved of him. Maybe you're starting to doubt the choice to bring him in on such a crucial role.

Maybe you're thinking about something totally different.

It's not for anyone else to know because we only see the mask. And really, few are going to see even that: Whenever they see you, all they'll see is your role, as invader.

Back to the meal and more importantly, the power drill.

The phone rests fully charged on the plate in front of victim #2. You better believe that she's thinking about it. You better believe victim #4 is staring at it.

What you aren't going to believe is what'll happen next.

You toy with victim #1, holding the power drill up to his ear, letting the sound of each pull cause him to tremble in fear. You make it count, building up the fear so that when you finally pierce his lower lip, it isn't just the wound that oozes fluid.

From the other room, invader shouts, "Did he just piss himself?!"

You nod.

Invader #2 laughs.

You look at the bay window again, the sunlight.

You pierce one of his earlobes and then, just because you start to get bored with the whole thing, you tear into his bicep. The drill has no trouble digging in and it leaves a deep, narrow, and circular cut that doesn't bleed until you apply pressure near the wound.

Say something like, Whoops. It slipped.

And then continue, this time the drill being aimed at victim #1's left eye.

It's a moment that would make anyone wince.

I almost don't believe it, that you're going to do something so risky, but then the camera moves in to get a better angle and it really does become one of those moments.

This is the sort of thing nobody can take from you.

Others have done this, but in this context, you create a scene that becomes as memorable as any good theatrical poster.

The cults are pleased.

I'm impressed too. I'll admit that I winced when the drill went so slowly into the eye.

How you held it there...

Letting it spin...

The human eye really does have fluid in it that can pour out if punctured. Sometimes you begin to question whether or not it's authentic, especially when some fictional presentations and analyses of performances exaggerate the details.

This is one of those scenes that'll be in the sample.

Victim #1 won't die from it, but at the same time, he won't be able to do much with such a grave affliction. From the other room, invader #2 shouts, "This means I can come back now, right?" You don't say anything and when he walks back in, he has to ask again, which isn't very professional. But no matter—he's there and because he's there, you hand him the power drill and tell him to clean it while you start on the wife.

Victim #1 looks like he's going to pass out.

For a moment, you wonder if he needs to be awake for this next part, but then—no, forget it. Might as well let him sleep it off.

Victim #2's blinks are slow and heavy, often shutting for ten, maybe fifteen seconds. Though victim #1 lost his eye, victim #2's the furthest from being able to fulfill anything but the most basic commands.

You talk to her, maybe.

I think you should talk to her, show a little bit of empathy.

Be different. Be ironic.

Fine. Don't. Just a thought is all. A suggestion.

Invader #2 returns, setting the power drill down on victim #3'a plate, a simple act that sends victim #2 into a full-bodied panic.

You have to hold down the chair just to keep it from falling.

Tell invader #2 to slap her across the face. But that doesn't help. Do it again. And again.

But the wife continues to flail and spasm.

If you were watching the television, you'd see that you're about to have another unexpected problem.

Victim #4 was able to free himself from his restraints. Somehow, the son was able to wear away the leather enough to free his hand. The camera captures the entire escape maneuver and I just want to say that, hey, I told you so. The kid has potential.

He grabs the cellphone from the plate and runs from the room.

You see it happen, but not until he's halfway across the room. Shout to invader #2, Well go fetch!

Victim #2 settles down almost immediately after the son's a room away.

You push the chair over, kicking the wife in the stomach.

Take one look at the unconscious husband before leaving the dining room. You need to know how this happened. You go right for the television. Good to see that you're learning. What's the camera capturing?

Where is the kid going?

Someone rings the front door. You jump to your feet.

Doorbell rings a second time, immediately followed by a third. Who could that be? The only thing that comes to mind is —yes, I think you're right.

No way.

It couldn't be…

I know, and worst possible timing.

Well look who it is—right on time, yet somehow the last thing you need right now. He doesn't seem to notice any differences between what's supposed to happen and what has instead become of the performance.

No, I'm not saying you've messed things up.

We already talked about this!

What's your motivation?

There you go.

Voice delivers the rehearsed, completely memorized lines —
"I'm the neighbor across the street and I noticed something odd
last night" and "I just wanted to check and make sure you were
okay."

He's an idiot. Plain and simple.

Be glad that the camera isn't watching. The cults won't see
this. No one will see this. How the hell is this a believable scene,
hmm? You have the voice posing as a neighbor talking to a
person who is obviously an invader, mask, dark clothing, blood
on the gloves. He's delivering the lines to the wrong person.
The only concession given is that he's on time. His version is
outdated. The performance has evolved to exceed his understanding.

Then he shouts, pretends to fall forward.

I'm guessing this is where one of your partners-in-performance was supposed to come up from behind and hit him
across the back of the head.

What an idiot.

Well, go ahead and drag him in.

He's going to play dead anyway.

You leave him playing dead in the foyer while you run back
to the television. The son is trying the phone. He's in a closet
somewhere. Now where's invader #2?

Invader #2 runs across the second floor hallway, a thin blade
in hand. He uses a lot of profanity, opting for more of a bullish
edge to flesh out his role.

"You little shit. I'm going to fucking find you."

What are you doing just sitting there?

"Come out, come out, come out you little fucker…"

The camera moves beyond invader #2 preferring to establish
a future shot, hanging low in the son's room, pointed towards
the closet where, you can imagine, the son is hiding. Why aren't
you running?

What's your motivation?

The voice isn't on the floor pretending to be unconscious.
Where did he go? Maybe you should turn your attention

toward finding the idiot but then I understand why you run upstairs. No one wants to have the last ten hours or so cut from the performance.

You trust me, right? So then when I tell you that you should go back and get a weapon, you'd listen to me, hmm? But you don't and you won't and when the voice shoots you with victim #4's .22 hunting rifle, you're not going to act surprised are you?
Didn't think so.

He got invader #2 in the arm. He's playing the role he's been assigned, keeping the weapon pointed on the closest of the two surviving invaders, you.
Invader #2 has his back pressed up against a wall just outside the son's room. He holds onto his left arm, head hanging low.
"Fucking piece of shit," he says.
You agree, of course.
As do I. But that's not going to stop it from happening.
The voice is nervous. As neighbor to the rescue, he has instantly gained victim #4's trust. He retrieves the phone, checking it to see if any calls were made, but what the cults won't realize until later is that one of you took the sim-card out.
Whose bright idea was that? Sure, you can claim it as your own.
He pockets it and tends to the son, saying things like, "We're going to get you some help" and "I can't believe this happened in our neighborhood. Our neighborhood is one of the safest in the entire country!"
He's terrible at acting but then again, it's believable enough. It sounds like he's nervous. Undoubtedly, he is more than a little unsettled.
I have to ask, while you're nursing that bullet-wound, how much of this was preplanned?
How much of this did you keep from me?
Remember when I said you shouldn't plan a performance all the way down to individual lines?
I knew he'd be a problem from the very beginning.

You knew that. And then you wrote out lines and a script for him because he was "nervous." It's good to be nervous.

Now you've got even more work to do.

You understand what I'm going to have to do now, right?

You've given me little recourse.

He'll be a mark, something forgettable, in your performance. He could have been worthwhile when now, his role is a mere waste.

With both invaders wounded, the voice and victim #4 return to the dining room to untie the rest of the family. The voice delivers various lines, the majority of them ill fitting for the situation. Victim #4 says something like, "We have to get out of here."

The voice loosens victim #2's restraints. She has difficulty standing up.

They run over to victim #1, who remains unconscious. Untied, four victims, four innocent individuals, faced with two assailants upstairs.

The son says, "We have to get out of here."

The wife asks, "Will you help us?"

A close-up shot of the voice's face; the look is one of notable alarm.

The cults wait to hear what the voice will say.

What's he going to say?

What's the next line in that script of yours?

"CALL THE POLICE."

AS IT TURNS OUT, the voice doesn't get to deliver that next line. Invader #5 made sure of it. It's a pretty little thing, this improvised scene. You've got the family, suddenly free and anxious to flee, and then you've got the voice, stumbling for a missing cue, a line that had to be his, but either he doesn't know how to improvise or is too stupid to take matters into his own hands. It ends the same way: Invader #5 walking in, double-tap to the chest with the fail-safe handgun I made sure he brought along for situations like this.

Experience tells you to be prepared.

Twin shots and the voice is a body floating in a puddle at the family's feet.

Invader #5 isn't supposed to shoot the family so instead gestures with his hand, "Call the police!" Then he points the gun at victim #4, "I said call the police." So they run, and you know where they're going to run. The camera doesn't follow, sticking instead with invader #5 before heading next door.

There's nothing else to see here.

Meanwhile…

Yeah, how are you doing? That shot to the shoulder, does it hurt real bad?

Invader #5 digs through the voice's pockets. No one's going to stop them. Invader #5 checks the phone and laughs.

Victim #2 turns and looks.

Invader #5 holds up the phone, shrugs and chucks it against the wall next to the wife, the phone shattering into a few pieces. That unsettles her. Victim #2 runs down the hall, headed for the stairs leading to the basement.

He waves, "See you soon!"

Invader #5 watches the television, doing precisely as what was directed. I merely need a moment to process how we'll fix this. It's not broken, not yet. However, at the same time, the spoilage is usually better controlled. I don't blame invader #1.

Invader #1 is new. There's potential in almost everyone as long as they don't let their emotions send them down directions that clearly won't end well.

But I identify a good enough cue. Much of what invader #1 had planned is a bust, simply not possible. But that's how this goes. I understood; in fact, I even told #1 that much of what is considered "the plan" would end up thrown out the window. Especially when the victims attempt to survive. If they don't, none of this is very interesting.

Hmm. It's one of those moments, you know?

"Yeah."

When the second act is complete and the cults are thinking everything's gone to hell. It's broken, the performance has that end of second act lull. There's typically a lull and it tends to happen around this time. Well, granted, it's usually because one of the key victims died, but this will have to do.

"They going to need some time?"

Yeah, I think invaders #1 and #2 will have to sit the next couple of scenes out.

"You're going to have to tell the guy. He doesn't get how it works."

I will. I wasn't told until after my partner-in-performance "accidentally killed" the kid, their only son. I didn't know that what I was being told was anything other than guidance from a mentor.

"True. That's how it works."

Exactly.

"So what's the deal?"

It's his first time. Second performances are cleaner.

"Shit yeah, look at all the blood."

But I like the first-time performances best. They're so different and unpredictable. For instance, did you expect me to send word this early?

"Actually I was setting up for a beer run, maybe some pizza. Was getting hungry over there. Didn't think it was happening anymore. I've seen plenty of bunch-a-fuckups."

I can fix this. I didn't expect the voice. But I can fix this.

"True."

Okay so I think it'll be easiest if you leave the body there until later.

"Yup."

You made sure that victim #3's watching, right?

"Yes sir."

Good. I'd like to have a word with her.

"She's not going anywhere."

No. Hmm, okay, so we've got the victims in the panic room. I had wondered why they didn't go for the room right from the beginning.

"It's a dud."

Excuse me?

"A dud—dead end, whatever."

Well, I made sure to have access, if it comes to it.

"Yeah, I watched it next door. Smart move."

Thank you. When you're forced to direct the performance, or at least as much of it based on the virtues of entertainment, you have to do what you can.

"You did that. You're doing that. I give you two thumbs up."

Thank you. Hmm, how about you go check on the others. I'll speak with victim #3. She must be so worried.

"She's doing better than the rest of her stupid family."

They're not stupid. They're playing their roles well.

"Call it what you want. They don't know what the hell's going on except we're the bad guys here to mess them up."

I'm more idealistic than that.

"I know, but then again, you've got a knack for this shit."

Like anything else, it's a performance. It's an act of expression.

And the most interesting and compelling acts catch the camera's attention.

The cults are watching. Always watching.

"They got nothing else to do."

We all need to be entertained.

The neighboring house is lit up as if the backup crew expected nightfall. The camera captures the best possible entrance into the house, if you were intending on entering unnoticed. Every room has been left untouched.

Pauses on the door to the basement, and if only because being here would have made it worth having a look, the camera descends the steps, entering a finished basement, complete with a long, labyrinthine hallway.

Enter one darkened room that exits into another.

The second room exits into a third.

Each room is smaller than the last until you come upon a door that doesn't look like the others. If you were to open that door, you'd see two bodies wrapped in black trash bags. You'd also see two children, quieted by a powerful dosage.

But it's a mere flicker of a scene, something that fits into the lull, the slow, brooding section before the final act of this performance takes hold.

Victim #3 is in the family room, sitting on the sofa, all restraints removed.

Invader #4 sits next to her, and if there weren't so late in the performance, you might have mistaken victim #4 for the daughter's mother. Or babysitter.

Yet that's precisely what invader #4 has told the daughter.

The daughter watches the television, ignorant to the factors at play.

Victim #3 smiles when she sees invader #5 pretending to be hurt in order to give invader #1 a hard time.

Victim #3 says, "He's being silly."

Invader #4 smiles, "He certainly is."

The faces blurred, the daughter doesn't seem to recognize invader #5.

Invader #4 says, "Do you want to watch something else?"

The daughter shakes her head, "This is okay."

"You're not tired of this?"

"No," the daughter doesn't look away from the television.

Invader #4 sighs, "You sure?"

She smacks her lips, "I like this."

The camera cuts to a close-up shot of invader #4 staring at the television, not amused, "Babysitter will be right back."

The daughter doesn't say anything, fully immersed in the performance.

"Want anything?"

Victim #3 says, "Umm..." then turns and looks at invader #4, "Some cereal?"

"You got it," invader #4 smiles.

Invader #4 walks into the kitchen, grabs a bowl out of one of the cabinets, milk from the fridge, cereal from the cupboard, and, before pouring anything, waits until we finish speaking. I figured given that it's the lull, I'd have a moment to check up on things.

How's victim #3?

Invader #4 exhales, "You saw her. I don't know what else to say."

I see. She seems to be... adjusting.

"Easy when the camera isolates reality from performance."

The blurred out faces help.

"Not just that, it's..." she hesitates, "never mind."

Tell me. You can trust me.

"Sure I can. But that's not the problem. I'm not in this for any other reason but the payday. I want this to work so that I can get paid. That's all it is to me."

Understandable. You and invader #5 were contracted for those reasons, nothing more. I don't expect you to be as enthusiastic as, say, invader #1.

"Yeah, and that's the real problem. You got a handle yet?"

I'm working on it.

"You got to tell. It's now or never."

You're right. Like I said to invader #5, I never knew until towards the end of my performance, but at the same time, I was more levelheaded. I didn't try to control everything. I lacked enough pride to do anything more than what was instructed by my mentor. I followed his lead, mostly because I had three houses to tackle.

"It could have been more if that partner of yours hadn't fucked up. The director had the idea to have it go on forever."

I know. It was really something.

And yet, the studio picked up on the thread and made it count on the silver screen.

"You failed though."

It was my first time.

"When are you going for another?"

Ah, I haven't yet decided.

"Well, you know my rate."

Thanks. I will keep you in mind.

"Sure you will."

I promise.

"Directors don't make promises unless they don't intend on keeping them. You pitch ideas. You present proposals."

I often forget why you are the way you are.

"I'm work-for-hire. Nothing but."

But you were once a part of your own performance.

"Yes," she pours the cereal.

"It didn't end well."

It opened doors for you. Sure, you didn't sell it to a studio. That's still a shame but—

"It didn't sell because our imbecile lead failed to produce enough interest on camera. It fell apart in the middle. Kind of like right now, actually."

Perhaps there's a similarity, yes. However, I wouldn't speak so lowly of the performance just yet. We have been given the opportunity to provide a powerful third act, wherein all roles are complete, the masks will be precisely what is expected.

"This is what I hate about the media."

I don't follow, is there a problem?

"Yeah. You tell me that my performance had potential but when I compare it with your beloved directorial debut, you shy away and take fault." She picks up a kernel of cereal and tosses it in her mouth, "You're a hypocrite."

Let's not get out of hand, especially not right now. Timing is everything. I must tell invader #1 or else his motivation will suffer.

Invader #4 rolls her eyes, "It's already suffered."

Even if that's the case, we are two-thirds into the performance. We have what will surely be a record that'll captivate every cult member. It could be great. I believe in it, fully. What's more, you have a role in the performance.

This will open more doors.

Invader #4 adds milk to the cereal, "Yeah, well, I'm not as easy to persuade as the others. Prove it to me. Like all your," she adds air-quotes to the following, "cult members." She leaves so that she might return to the camera. I remain, like the performance as a whole: potentially ruined.

It all comes down to whether or not I can capture invader #1's attention.

Invader #4 stops and looks over her shoulder, "If anyone had any real guts, they wouldn't hide behind the camera anymore. They'd come right out and say it. They'd say: 'Yeah, it's me.' 'Yeah, it's us.' It's not a cult if it encompasses an entire nation. Everyone's watching. Everyone's a victim. Everyone's looking for something to gain. Fame does that."

Invader #4 pauses, searching for the right words, and then says:

"Never forget the importance of entertainment."

A cheap shot, for sure, and yet I let it go. For this is all behind the scenes, footage that's not recorded. The camera is elsewhere. One look at the television in the other room and its clear. I'm not here and never was. If it isn't a part of the performance, if it isn't part of the final record, it doesn't exist. This conversation doesn't exist.

Much like my discussion with invader #5, it's material entirely for a director's purposes. But even so, that really was a cheap shot.

What makes it hurt is the fact that she's right.

Above the cults and the craft, the camera and the performance, it begins and ends with entertainment. We want to be entertained. That's all this is, anyway.

That's all it ever was and will ever be.

A product, and production, of entertainment.

At the end of the lull is a scene that brings everything back up to speed. You wrap the wound with a bandage initially meant for the voice, but he's dead and, by the look of it, you don't seem to be upset. Invader #5 removes the bullet from invader #2's arm.

Invader #2 shouts, "Motherfucker, that hurts."

Invader #5 says, "You were shot. It would be fucked up if it didn't hurt."

You watch your partners-in-performance, eyeing #5 in particular.

I know what you're thinking.

I understand what this must feel like to you, at this precise moment. But you don't say anything. Not at first.

You stare at the voice's body.

Invader #5 notices and points at the dead body, "I killed him."

Say something like, Yes you did.

But now you're not listening to me. You don't say anything.

You don't do anything but because the camera holds on you, it's evident that you are in the process of changing this. No, I don't know what it is. You haven't told me. I am not doing anything.

Look, walk into the other room.

Away from the camera.

Do what you must but afterward…

We need to talk.

CHAPTER
SEVENTEEN

NOW THAT WE'RE on level ground, what does the camera see?

All three invaders sit on the couch, watching television.

Onscreen, it's the daughter. The daughter is watching herself finish a bowl of cereal. There's invader #4 taking the bowl, leaving the room.

Then it's all three invaders, sitting on the couching watching themselves watching back, looking for direction.

The panic room.

You need to get into that room.

The panic room is unpredictably in the basement rather than upstairs, adjacent and/or connected to one of the bedrooms. The idea of a panic room is to be there so that the victim doesn't have to cross paths with any and all invaders. A couple feet from the bed and then, once inside, you're safe. Or at least you think you're safe.

There are ways into panic rooms, but none of them are what you would expect.

The thing about a panic room, what really sells it as a mainstay among the rural well-to-do is that it is impossible to break into from the outside.

It's impossible to break in and it's impossible to escape.

Without a number of innovative and "creative" countermeasures, the victim remains secure in the panic room.

There is no other cause for panic except for the invaders that may suffer a completely spoiled performance.

If you're listening, I'll direct you. Are you listening?

What's your motivation?

First of all, the camera is your best bet. Have one of the invaders sit upstairs, watching the television. I suggest it being invader #2 because he's 1) injured and 2) less likely to contribute to the scene than invader #5.

"I fucking resent that," invader #2 interrupts.

That's too bad. How unfortunate.

If invader #1 agrees, I believe we need to move in a direction other than at a stalemate. Because this is, in fact, our current situation.

We are outside, out of reach.

The family is inside, unable to contact the outside world, sure, but still. This looks bad. Really bad.

"Fuck," invader #2 winces, gripping his arm.

Invader #5 says, "Yeah well you were shot."

Invader #1 doesn't say anything.

It's up to the possibilities.

What are the possibilities? Tell me and then I'll tell you. You trust me, right? Yeah, well a good director collaborates with his lead, his producers. We're here to make history, to completely baffle the cults. We'll settle for a solid thumbs up from the cults.

"The fucking critics don't give a shit," invader #2 shouts.

They do. They've been interested in this brand of material for decades. It's only now that we're seeing a surge, a climb to fame.

Popular culture wants something real.

Their entertainment must be real.

Realer than real. And you know what that means…

Yes. Precisely. Their entertainment must make the cults uncomfortable. It must unsettle, absorb, curate obsession. It must be as close to being a tale written for them, a piece of media made to spoil only their chances of being able to change the future.

That's what the studio wants.

That's what the media wants.

"That's what we want," invader #5 says.

So you think you can persuade them to exit the panic room? How?

Well, you need to know how.

You can't just spitball ideas. The victims are hurt and likely to lose consciousness sooner rather than later. If they pass out or die, the performance dies.

Okay, I'll tell you of the initial possibilities.

The one I've seen time and time again, although it works only in fifty percent of scenarios, involves beckoning the victims to escape. I'll explain—

One performance involved pets. It's unsettling, but it was necessary.

And it made for a hell of a performance. That scene, it gets me just thinking about it. More or less, what the invaders did was they took the dog and stood their ground outside of the panic room door. They proceeded to harm the dog, mistreating it in a variety of ways, many of them causing the poor defenseless dog to whimper and buckle, collapsing to the floor. That didn't work. It wasn't enough. It took some physical kicks to get the victims' attention and a subsequent hurl of the dog against a wall to get the wife to open the panic door, as if she had what it took to save the dog.

She wasn't able to save her own self.

Another example involved the pilfering and destruction of a family's expensive collections of jewelry, books, and other creature comforts. This took time. I don't remember how long. I'd say a few days. More than what you have, mind you.

The invaders narrated the entire looting, frequently returning to where the victims could see and watch, holding up the item(s) and asking about the worth, possible value on the resale market. When they ran out of stuff to steal, they started breaking the more priceless items. I remember they got to the point where they were burning important documents, photo albums, and other material, having a bonfire right there in that bedroom, shooting at the smoke detector when it went off.

Truly an amusing series of scenes.

Hmm? Oh, the father opened the door, willing to die if it meant saving his precious masterwork. Not a novelist. It was some file for a lawsuit or something. It had money written all over it. The father would rather die than let all that work go to waste.

It's interesting to see how people will react.

More so, it's entertaining to watch and find out what that "something" will be that breaks a person, rendering them subservient.

If not this, how about...

This one's unlikely but the one performance I've seen wherein the invaders chose to use toxic gas, in their case, they rigged up a car with a long hose, shoved it into the nearby adjourning vent, blocked the external vent that lets escape any and all carbon monoxide, and they had at it. One of the invaders sat in the car jamming to heavy metal, bobbing his head up and down, that mask he was wearing making it look silly. The whole thing. A clown rocking to heavy metal while using the blade in his hand as a fake guitar.

A poisonous substance will definitely work.

You run the risk of killing the victims before they can escape, but at the same time, the fight or flight response is usually strong in victims if they managed to make it into the panic room unscathed; chances are they never thought, even for one split second, that they had a chance. They fled rather than fought.

You'll need a vehicle. They've got three in their garage.

You'll have to drive it up to where the panic room is located.

You'll have to find the external ventilation; also, you will need to map out how all the vents are connected. Yes, it will take some time.

It will take a lot of work.

Perhaps more than is left in the performance.

We're at a lull, that moment in the performance where the

big final act, full of violence and blunt kills, is a few scenes away and we're stitching together the scraps left behind from the two previous acts. We're looking for that one item that'll linger, that one piece of information, that one scene, that gets them out of the panic room.

If not this, how about…

Well, it's not something we'd be able to do but I'll mention it. You can wait until they die. Really, that's happened before. Yes. It did.

What's better is that a studio picked it up.

It didn't garner a huge amount of attention, but the end result produced a fair amount of success. The cults watched. The cults liked.

But they didn't love.

There was only one invader left. He had a partner but that one took, I think, a number of stabs to the back. Yeah, that one victim, the son, he played a lot of videogames. The kid was completely desensitized.

The remaining invader messed up and couldn't get to the family in time. They got into their panic room but couldn't dial out because they didn't have a room with its own panel. The panic room was just a room. They didn't have food in there either.

The invader knew what he had to do.

So brought a chair up to the front of the panic room, putting his feet up on the wall that slid into place over the panic room door.

He waited. He read a book.

Meanwhile the camera captured what happened in the panic room.

It was unsettling. Long, seemingly endless hours of a father bleeding out slowly, the wife, son, and younger son, doing their best to keep him alive.

They had a one-year-old that broke his leg earlier in the performance.

The one-year-old wasn't as willing as the rest of the family.

The one-year-old panicked and became claustrophobic.

They didn't know that the one-year-old had asthma.

They knew about three hours in. The wife couldn't bear to live with seeing her young child die in her arms. So she died too.

Then the younger son.

The father, it turns out, held out longer than imagined.

The son, the one that had killed the other partner, sat in a panic room full of death for another three before he fell asleep.

He didn't wake back up. It's as if he willed himself into death.

I kid you not. It happened.

You'll have to track down the performance. It's one of the more obscure ones, these days. After the family died, the invader knew because the camera knew and he just stood up, removed the mask, changed into the father's clothes, burned his, along with the mask and the role, and he walked the neighborhood streets, waving to neighbors, neighbors waving back, to the nearest strip mall where he had parked his car.

I don't think the invader has collaborated on another performance.

It was a one-off, straight shot. Some only need one. At least they got one.

If the invader could do it again—or someone else, because it doesn't have to be this invader—I'd love to see a performance where the invaders can just sit and wait patiently until they die, perhaps tormenting them psychologically, but that's not you and that's not for me to decide.

No it would be different because they'd intentionally do it.

They'd get them in the panic room, have it all planned out, the broadstrokes, not every single action, yeah, I had to mention that. What's your motivation?

Okay, okay, but what I was saying had to do with a whole performance that takes place under static conditions. The invaders smoke, play games, talk, drink, hang out outside while they psychologically torment the family that lives, for a time, in the panic room. Idea would be that the invaders would have known how to disable communication with the outside world. Maybe they'll turn the power on and off in the panic room, long enough so that the victims get used to one condition before being handed its opposite.

It could be a good performance.

Low maintenance, high planning. The casing on this would require a lot more than what was needed for this performance. Additionally, it would be of interest to the cults, especially those with a lot of experience with the craft, to see the invaders living, I mean really living, eating, watching television, on the computer, living in the victims' home while they remain captive in a small-contained space.

Ideas get around. Hope this one holds.

If not this, then how about...

Sadly this is the most common method. It is also the method that never works. It worked once, I believe, in a failed perfor-mance, only because the victims got tired of hearing all the drilling and sounds ricocheting through the vents, seeping in and getting under their skin. Horrible condition to be in, forced to hear the relentless banging and clanging of invaders' that won't give up. It's not in an invader's role to give up.

Not the good ones anyway.

But to stay on point, you could give it all you got.

Chip away at the wall. It's dry wall for the first part, then you'll see the steel, whatever the panic room exterior chassis is made of, and it will undoubtedly cause some panic for you, the invader, because you'll know that it'll take a lifetime to get through it.

Well, there's another way.

Not just the physical attacking from all sides; rather, you could work on rewiring the electrical slider, the part of the panic room that locks the door into place.

But you need someone with prowess, someone that can do the impossible, with engineering experience.

Does invader #2 have what it takes?

"Fuck you," invader #2 shouts, which sends another sharp pain up his arm.

If he were capable, he would have already realized that speaking, much less shouting would increase the pain. So then it's pretty obvious that he hasn't and that he isn't capable of doing any reverse engineering.

Then it's the method that's most definitely not happening.

So then how about…

If you had someone, say that voice character, still alive and not stupid and useless in his undoing of what could have been an extremely interesting second half of the performance, you could have planted him in the panic room with the family. Posing as someone that helped, you could have had him open the door from the inside.

Clean and simple.

But then again that's not going to happen.

It's a shame that the backup crew won't be able to perform as planned.

A double crew attacking the same house on the same night…

It's marvelous.

I believe it's been done, yes, but not at this capacity.

There was the one performance that involved kidnapping the victims, binding them to odd sub performances, typically acts of survival based on their willingness to take on the pain and punishment that'll be dealt in order for them to survive.

There was the one woman that woke up with an apparatus on her head.

Umm, it was a bear trap in reverse, so that the part that retracts was in her mouth. She would be given some time to escape but if she messed up, the apparatus would engage, causing her jaw, and most of her face, to slice open.

Gruesome image. But it's one of the most successful performances in the history of the craft. We're talking a number of adaptations, given that the invasion wasn't a home; it had undergone a new approach. The invaders invaded homes and residences and pulled the victims into their own, preplanned environments. Privacy shattered like anything else, it became a performance draped in fear.

It's uncanny, a true anomaly.

Huh? Right—the invader remained in the room with the victims the entire time, posing as a dead body.

Another instance: One that did not end well due to the family turning on the invader, systematically torturing and killing her instead of it being, as intended, the other way around. The invader posed as a relative that the family hadn't seen in a long time. The invader did her research, going to great lengths to understand the relationship of said relative and each family member. She showed up one night needing help. They took her in of course. It would have been weird if it were anyone else but the relative had a history of drug abuse and had stayed with the family for a spell once before.

A day after arriving, she turned on them, drugging the food she had prepared for them to express her gratitude. They woke up in a room with her, but, ironically, her downfall, her biggest mistake, was that the real relative showed up with the same issue—needing sanctuary for a time—and the family and real relative worked to dispatch of the invader, hurting her and punishing her before ending her life.

It's an interesting one, for sure. The performance exists, the record is out there, for any and all to see. The trick is that it's not commercial. It hasn't been exhibited to the cults wide and varied. It remained somewhat of an insider record.

I think it had to do with the lawyers.

It puts the family in a bad light. The record got out though.

It always does. Some try to hide it, especially if they are unsatisfied with their performance, but it always finds a way.

Everything ends up in the hands of someone willing to watch, hoping to be entertained. Hmm. Again, it's a shame.

If everything had gone according to plan, you wouldn't be in this situation. You clearly didn't think much of something like this happening. A remote possibility.

What were the chances? You've got to agree that it's a little amusing.

If even just a little. The one thing that didn't seem possible:

Bam, it happened.

But spoilage turns things around, giving the planned and maybe predictable a new spin. I know I've got plans. Do you?

Well, you'll just have to see. Again, I can't tell you everything.

If you know everything you won't be interesting to the camera.

Ultimately there are other possibilities, many of which

require different minds, completely difference circumstances to generate and put into practice.

Ultimately you have the one choice, the one you'll choose.

Which one will you choose?

What's your motivation?

"WHAT DO THEY WANT FROM US?"

WHAT'S THEIR MOTIVATION? What keeps a family from falling apart? What keeps a family branded as victims from victimizing each other, blaming one, blaming all, before letting the events transpiring destroy them for good?

What does the camera see?

Invader #2 watches.

Victim #3 watches.

Invader #4 watches the daughter watching her family, unaware of what is about to occur, the reveal that, perhaps, the daughter already knew: it's her family.

The camera sits with the family as they face the alarming facts of their role.

The husband says, "I'm a victim."

The wife says, "I'm a victim..."

The son chokes and then whispers, "I'm a victim."

The camera sits in place for the daughter, and it might be that it sits there, in the half circle alongside the rest of the family, as a subliminal message to the viewer, one that says: *You could be a victim too.*

In varying states of disrepair, the family's worst wounds are deep inside, the dreaded fact that they know. They know how this goes. Their role, as victims, is to not know, but in actuality, they understand what's happening.

Victim #1's seen a performance or two long before it ever spread across all medial channels and inevitably became part of popular culture.

Victim #2 has never viewed any, not even the pop culture sensations. She doesn't keep up with popular culture. Most of the time, she spends her time keeping up with the items in her life that she's never been able to acquire.

Victim #3 is watching one right now. Her own.

Victim #4 won't tell his parents but he's seen one. A friend from school got a hold of a recent record, one of a performance that happened two houses down. They watched it and drank beers. There were six of them, hanging out on a Friday night. Though they all thought it was intense and unsettling, by the end they were all taking bets, turning the record into a drinking game.

Between small scenes that involve a sequence of dialog between the family members, they default to their dejected, harmed look, the look of a victim.

The camera maintains the same shot the entire time; it never moves. It never switches shots. The scene is one long scene. It lengthens towards the early evening, the last evening of their lives.

A continuous shot to be viewed later by the cults as something of a meditation on the lives they will never get to lead.

It is also a bonding experience.

For each family member, by the end, will apologize to each other. Perhaps it won't be an apology, but everything will be put on the table.

Everything hidden will be set down on a place.

What do they want from us?

The answer is simple. Figuring out how to not let them get

what they want... that's different. But it takes everything, a family's collective effort, to shut out the answer.

Instead, they pick through the small stock of rations.

They sit on the floor in the same half-circle, each with a paper plate, plastic fork, and a variety of preserved foods.

They must be hungry.

But it's surprising because they don't eat.

Instead they hold their forks and they pick at something else.

Victim #1 as a father says to the son, "Did you ever finish recording that album?"

The son doesn't appear to be surprised. Then again, the father is accustomed to forgetting important moments in his family's life. For a short duration, no longer than a summer, the father forgot that he had a son.

Not blatantly, mind you, but they never crossed paths. In all of three months, they walked, lived, and breathed lives that had little to do with the other.

But here, the father remembered something.

The son says, "Yeah."

"That's great!"

The father's reply is genuine.

The son sighs, "I guess. The band broke up."

Nothing else is said.

The father looks at the fork in his hand.

The son does the same.

It seemed to be enough.

Victim #2 as wife asks the husband, "Was it me?"

The husband inhales, holding it in, thinking about what to say. The wife looks at the one eye he has left, the other a mess of drying blood and a slow drip of fresh blood that ends up on his shirt, disregarded.

"It was everything. Me, you, the job."

The wife looks at the knife in her shoulder, "I've tried to see other people."

The husband looks at the son but the son doesn't look back. This isn't about him. He watches, like the daughter, invader #2, and invader #4 watches. They watch it plain, the sort of scene that extends longer than is necessary but the viewer doesn't seem to notice. It's the personality and humanity of the role(s) that buoys the entire scene.

He says, finally, "I don't expect you to be faithful if I'm not."

The wife runs a finger around the base of the knife, "I tried to but it's not the same. It feels... different."

The husband understands. He nods.

The wife says, "I forgive you. But you have to forgive me."

The husband smiles, "I forgive you."

The wife tries to smile, "I forgive you."

Victim #4 as son says to the mother, "I'm sorry too."

The mother looks away from the knife, tilting her head, "What about, honey?"

But of course she knows.

The fact that she pretends that it wasn't a problem said everything.

The son looks at the fork.

The mother looks at the son.

The camera catches a smile.

Victim #4 as son talks to the father about this girl he met online. He talks about how they get along, not because they like the same things but because they don't like anything. They have things that they care about but mostly they talk about what's missing in their lives. They obsess over how everything is messed up and then the son stops, makes a face, and then realizes that they do have something in common:

They like that they hate everything.

The father listens intently.

The son stops and pretends to snap his fingers.

He doesn't due to the wounds inflicted.

The father looks at the son's hand.

You can see the blood.

You can see the effects of blood-loss on their faces.

The son is starting to become delirious.

He loses track of what he was talking about. However, that's not the reason why he's talking. The father listens intently, not

at all interested but still, he listens. He likes that he has to listen.
He is the son's father; he needs to make an effort.

The son gives the father that chance.

If only just this once.

Victim #1 as husband says to the wife, "I tried to replace
you."

He wants to get it out there, despite how horrible it'll sound.

"That's what I was doing with the other women. I just…"

The husband whimpers, his pain becoming severe.

The wife says, "Take your time."

It takes him a minute.

It's evident that what keeps the family talking is the fact that
they might have another chance.

The pain subsides enough to ignore that there's any pain
at all.

He continues, "You reminded me of my age. I'm a kid. I've
never grown up. I react like a kid reacts. When something bad
happens I run away. I run away from you. I'm still running. But
now I'm tired."

The husband looks at her, really looks at her, eye to eye:

"I'm tired."

The wife says tiredly, "Come home."

Outside, the sun sets on the second day. There are only a few
hours left.

The family, for a time, cannot bear to move. They remain
frozen in place, eyes shut, the effects of their roles causing the
occasional sound of pain swelling, causing a cough, a wince, a
devastating charge of panic.

But the family continues to perform their roles.

They don't say what they want to say.

They hold back.

They won't say it.

They won't say: *I'm going to die.*

The husband talks about his job. He prefaces it by saying, "I know that you don't care. It's okay. I hate my job. I'm the one that cares the least."

"Then why didn't you quit?" asks the son.

"I had to support the family."

The wife says, "Thank you."

There was no reason to thank victim #1, but victim #2 did, for the one and only reason: The wife understood how much of his life he sacrificed to pay the bills. She didn't want to work but hid it under the idea of being unable to work.

Besides, it wasn't an issue given how much her husband made.

But it was, and had been the source of many arguments.

Not that the arguments directly referenced the work situation.

But it was there. It was obvious that the husband loathed his job. And in time, it caused him to move away from her.

Victim #1 looks at victim #2 but doesn't say anything.

The words—thank you—are what he had wanted to hear all along, but didn't realize until now, until it was too late.

Victim #1 wants to hug victim #2. Victim #1 wants to kiss victim #2.

Victim #2 wants to hug victim #1. Victim #2 wants to kiss victim #1

Victim #4 wants to hug victims #1 and #2. Victims #1 and #2 want to hug victim #4.

The victims want to know what happened to victim #3. They look at the camera, where the daughter should have been, but see nothing.

Victim #2 as mother says into the camera, "Sweetie, I'm so, so, sorry." As if she is responsible for the performance, the mother apologizes for everything that's happened.

She tries to cry but there are no tears left.

She tries to move but her body won't let her.

The son offers to help but he can't move either.

Blood has pooled where he sits.

The family notices, and it's that sort of notice that breaks them all down into what little of them was left. They are victims.

This is a performance.

If they could be remembered as anything else, they would choose to be the flawed family they were before this happened.

Victim #1 as father says into the camera, "Honey, where are you?"

He pauses, bringing a hand to his face, up to his mutilated eye, but stops right before touching it, understanding how much pain will be felt if he touches it.

He says, "Honey…"

There's nothing else to say.

Victim #4 as brother says into the camera, "If you can hear us, see us, if you're anywhere where you can escape, please do it! I hope, I hope…"

There should be tears but, same as with victim #2, there is only excruciating, debilitating pain.

The family says it all at once, "Run."

And then they stare at the camera, where the daughter would have been sitting.

There's nothing left to say.

Somber moments like these are so effective that even invader #2 ignores his own pain for a moment to enjoy the pain of others.

The family starts breathing in and out in unison.

Breathe in. Hold.

Breathe out. Release.

Their breaths have become panicked. They can't seem to think straight.

Victim #1 starts, "I think we'll…" but can't finish the sentence.

Victim #2 looks at her fork.

Victim #4 looks at the camera.

This time, perhaps, he sees it staring back at him, filming everything.

The family breathes in.

Breathes out.

How many more will they get?

Outside the panic room, the family watches from the panel display invader #1 walking into the room, walking up to where the door would be, if it weren't hidden behind a retracting wall. Invader #1 looks up at them, at the small little dot in the wall, the security camera. Invader #1's mask no longer frightens them.

Fear has become the only feeling they know.

It's better than feeling pain.

The family breathes in, breathes out. It's going to end soon.

They know that it is. Without mentioning it, they appear to accept their roles. Maybe they accepted them a long time ago, much longer than your choice to invade their home. A home invasion, of sorts, culminates a long-running fracture in the so-called stability of this home, this family.

The camera is deliberate and intent on maintaining the single shot.

If it had switched shots, invader #1's mask would have been seen for what it truly was, a role, a simple mask made to evoke a trickle of discomfort.

Instead everyone's faces are blurred.

Much like how the family's eyesight will begin to blur before facing what might be, for them, the final scene.

The family breathes in and breathes out. They look down at their paper plates. They look at each other. This could be their last meal.

Victim #1 is the first to cut a piece from the meat byproduct.

Victim #2 follows his lead.

Victim #4 directs his fork to a slice of peach, soaked in a syrupy sauce.

They look at each other.

It could be just another meal, maybe. They do their best to treat it as such.

Victim #1 breathes in. He breathes out and then takes a bite.

Hard to swallow, and there's no water in the panic room, he chews slowly.

Victim #2 breathes in. She breathes out and takes in a forkful.

She chews faster than the husband but doesn't swallow until victims #1 and #4 take their second bites.

Victim #4 breathes in. He breathes out and puts the entire peach in his mouth. He swallows it in one bite.

This concludes the single shot, cutting abruptly to the other house.

Invader #4 sits back down with the daughter and says, "Do you like this show?"

The daughter shakes her head, "No."

"Why not?"

"Because it's almost over."

Invader #4 offers to change the channel.

The daughter resists, "I want to know what happens."

"It's a sad ending."

The daughter shrugs, "I want to know."

Invader #4 leans back, stretching, "I imagine it won't last much longer."

The daughter looks at invader #4 and says, "I'm a victim too."

Everything is laid bare, no matter how bold, private, and embarrassing.

The family listens and the family understands.

They have to. They won't be given a second chance.

The one heartwarming moment is shattered when they see her on the panel display.

If there had been any doubt, the family could at least enjoy the knowledge that she is still alive.

Now they could all die together, as a family.

CHAPTER
NINETEEN

A DOMESTIC SWELL. I imagine it's more or less the equivalent of what this is, the moment when the family discovered that victim #3 had yet to finish up her role in the performance. She's still here. She's been watching the entire time. The swell of both joy and fear coalesced when the daughter walking into frame trailed behind by invader #4, who held her hand as if she were the real mother.

A domestic swell followed by a collapse, the final collapse.

All participants in the performance can sense it…

I can see it forming from a fourth, undeclared vantage point, the one behind the camera. A domestic swell: the occurrence of safety becoming a stage, the realization that no one is safe. Not that they ever were.

Here we go…

Victim #3 listens to what you tell her. You say something like, Wave to your parents. Make sure they see you. Do they see you?

The daughter nods, "I think so."

You check with invader #2, who replies, "Of course. Why even ask?"

But you know as well as anyone the importance for setting precedence, letting the pieces fall into place. They see her. They acknowledge that you have the upper hand.

You say something like, So then who wants the first hug?

The camera sticks to where you stand, which means you've got it right. The tone is more or less perfect. Now how about capitalizing on it?

Here's what you do—

Provoke them. I know you did but keep going.

Offer the first hug and, because the cults already understand that the victims can't communicate directly with you, everything you say and do will be answered in silence unless they are able to leave the panic room.

Say, Anyone?

Say, We're so sorry that we've kept her, she's been busy. But don't you worry now, she's seen everything!

Say, But she's back! And she wants a hug.

Say, Who wants a hug?

There are only two possible answers—silence or the sound of the panic room door sliding open. Unsurprising then when you hear nothing, the sort of silence that fills in the space between breaths.

Say, Nobody?

Let there be a pause. Trust me.

Then let invader #4 hug her first.

But not before saying, Your family doesn't want to say hello? Now that's just mean. Hold it all in for a second and then shout, Well don't feel bad!

Glance over at invader #4, who already understands what to do, and say, Cheer her up, why don't you?

Invader #5 hands invader #4 a knife.

Invader #5 tells the daughter to "Cheer up."

Invader #4 nods, "They're frightened is all. You must be frightened too."

Say something like, Are you afraid?

Victim #3 shakes her head, "No."

Invader #4 says, "You're not. My you're a brave little girl."

Invader #5 doesn't say anything. Hmm, actually, we might as well utilize all of our resources. How about, saying something contradictory to what the other invaders are posing? It's up to you. I have no preference.

That could be good.

Yes. I agree.

So then, have him whisper it into the daughter's ear.

Invader #5 takes a knee. The camera zooms in close, both of their faces filling the frame. Invader #5 waits until the daughter can feel his warm breath on her ear before delivering the line you had in mind: "You should be."

The daughter turns and grabs invader #4's leg.

Instead of returning the gesture, invader #4 lets go of the daughter's hand and pushes her to the ground.

You try to cheer her up, She didn't mean it. Really she didn't.

Oh don't be that way...

Victim #3 screams, "No!" When you attempt to help her onto her feet.

You look back at the panic room security camera.

Invader #5 grabs victim #3's hand. No matter what the daughter does to try to break free—kicking, screaming, biting— invader #5 tightens the grip on her hand.

He laughs, "Did you really think she was the babysitter?"

You laugh.

Invader #2 laughs. Everyone can hear him from the basement.

There is laughter prior to the knowledge settling in that the scene, that scene, the one where the begging begins and the bloodshed is most final, is upon us.

I have to admit that I'm both nervous and excited. Yes, as much, if not more, than you are. It's a good thing. It means we'll get it on camera.

What's your motivation?

What's your motivation?

What's your motivation?

It's this moment. Everything that came before it can pass on by; this is it.

This is where you end the performance. Like completing the perfect statement, you are about to do just that: A final scene to finish off the somber act that was the last night. This night. Your night. Our night.

It's worth noting what the camera never captured. It's worth noting how the family watched the small tiny panel display as the daughter became the primary victim of torture. And it wasn't anything physical, just a few words, and some laughter.

But it was right there, when the daughter screamed, that victim #1 began shaking. Victim #2 closed her eyes. She couldn't bear to watch.

Victim #4 vomited, and the vomit dribbled from his mouth but he didn't move. He didn't look away. They sat where they sat and watched.

You see, they wanted to move:

Victim #1 would rather die than watch the invaders harm the young girl. His daughter.

Victim #2 would rather be the one under the knife, the one dismantled and violated, than see the invaders harm the young girl. Her daughter.

Victim #4 would rather fight or die trying than see the invaders harm the young girl. His sister.

Their daughter. Their only daughter.

His sister. His only sister.

But they couldn't move.

How do we know this? How do we know what isn't captured on camera? We know it because of one particular item I kept from you.

Consider it a testament to contingency plans.

You didn't fare well during that test; mind you, the anxiety and power trip of assuming lead in a performance often dispels and destroys spontaneity and the ability to maintain control. It's ironic when the very reason why you do what you do becomes the one reason why it'll become the death of you.

But that's why I'm here. That's why you contacted me.

You needed direction.

Well, I'm your director.

As your director, I present to you, the key to the panic room.

Let him walk it off. He'll need help. He hasn't moved a muscle for a long time.

Invader #3 took a shot to the leg for the performance.

If I ask him—

What's your motivation?

He'd have his own reasons. And yet, they're all the same.

We all do it for the same reasons. Perhaps we phrase it differently, but in the end we do it to entertain and be entertained.

Anything else is extraneous.

Invader #3 presses the gun against victim #4's forehead, opting for the youngest of the three, based entirely on the principles of persuasion.

If a child is in danger, the parent will do whatever's necessary to achieve safety for its kin. Invader #3 coughs, looking into victim #1's lone eye, shaking his head as if to say: Don't even try it. Invader #3 turns his attention to victim #2 but her eyes are closed.

He whistles.

He gets her attention.

He steps on one of the son's wounded hands while pointing the gun at victim #2, "Tell her to wake the fuck up."

No one moves.

"I said tell her to pay attention."

When the wife opens her eyes, the camera catches up, cutting direct to a shot for shot reveal of the barrel of the gun, point blank, on the wife's forehead, invader #3 pressing into her flesh hard enough to leave a mark.

You can see it when invader #3 aims the gun at the son.

Invader #3 says, "Open sesame."

No one moves.

No one says anything.

Invader #3, visibly annoyed, shouts, "Open the fucking door!"

We're all watching from the other side.

Invader #2 can't believe it, "Shit, you think you know somebody..."

That's just it. Everyone wears more than one role, even if they decide to wear the same mask, they are playing a number of roles, capable of baking more than a few pies.

194 MICHAEL J. SEIDLINGER

Invaders #1 through #5, and everyone in between, the cults and the stride itself, inching towards the moment when everyone finally meets in the one room for one final and most interesting display, everyone is watching.

Everyone is ready for this to end.

Invader #3 cocks the gun, "I said open the door."

The tone is flat and severe.

Invader #3 says, "I'm not going to ask again... open the fucking door."

Victim #2 stumbles forward, crawling towards the panel, towards the one button press that'll push us towards forty-eight hours complete.

"No," invader #3 shakes his head, "let's have the pants-wearer do it."

You can see it on his face: Victim #1's heart sinks.

"This is *your* family, isn't it? *Your* family. *Your* house. *Your* property. *Your* privacy. *Your* concept of the household, *your* home, as an institution, should be?"

Victim #1 tries to speak, "I..."

"I want you to open the door."

Victim #2 reaches for the button. The door slides open.

Hey, wait—let's... see this out.

Yeah, let's give invader #3 a chance to sniff out this lead.

Don't walk in. This is invader #3's scene.

Invader #3 shakes his head, "Close the door."

Victim #2 says, "Please... don't do this..."

"I said... close. The. Door."

The button is pressed. The door closes.

The camera captures the pull of the trigger.

Victim #4's head caves in on one side, the splatter of brain matter and dark shards of his skull paint the left side of the panic room. Jesus, that was loud.

You okay? Invader #3's fine. He had earplugs on.

The gun is pointed at victim #2, invader #3 shouts, "She going to be next?!"

Victim #1 can't move. His attempt sends him to the floor. Victim #2, distraught, her son just died, helps victim #1 to his feet.

"No," invader #3 shakes his head. "He's going to do this on his own. Play by *his* principles. Or are those not your principles, hmm?"

Victim #1 can't speak. He can't move.

It's a miserable image, the father pulling his defeated body forward.

Victim #2 watches, feeling absolutely useless. She chews on her lower lip. She bites down so hard that she begins to tear into the lip.

Invader #3 leans on the one good leg of his, "Come on, come on, come on! We don't have all day! We still have to kill you all!"

In five minutes, though not with a lack of effort, giving it everything he's got, the sum of a life of familial neglect and disregard, victim #1 has only made it halfway across the room. He won't make it to the panel, the button. But then perhaps he knows. And yet, for the sake of never having tried before, he tries now, to protect and save his family.

Invader #3 sighs, "Fuck it," and stumbles over to victim #1, ending his role right then and there. Invader #3 presses the button.

He looks at victim #2 and shrugs, "Times up."

Invaders #4 and #5 are the first to step inside the panic room. Invader #5 grabs victim #1's body while invader #4 grabs the son's body. They drag out the bodies, laying them out on a prepared area, where plastic has been laid out.

Victim #2 is held at gunpoint by invader #3 until further specified.

Victim #3 sits cross-legged next to you, watching it all happen.

A blank expression on her face.

Invader #2 descends the basement stairs with the sack of tools and a white tin containing an unknown substance. Everyone gets to be involved in this scene.

Invader #3 and victim #2 are the last to exit the panic room. Victim #2 is told to sit next to her daughter. You tell them not to acknowledge each other.

Say something like, You had your chance to show affection.

You stay with them, the gun handed back to you, a brief but well-deserved nod of respect shared between you and #3. Not a moment is wasted.

Invaders #2 and #3 remain in the basement, their injuries, though minor, will only complicate things.

Invaders #4 and #5 head upstairs, tending to the voice's body.

The body is placed next to victims #1 and #3.

Now that everyone is present, the camera pans out, tending to a full panorama of the scene. It's at this moment that it's yours, your chance to speak, and I mean really speak. There's nothing left, no reason to hold back.

As director, I ask you:

What's your motivation?

As an invader, you answer:

To be entertained.

Your voice is my voice.

The rest of the answer is the scene that unfolds.

You tell victims #2 and #3 to beg for their life.

They don't beg for their life.

Victim #3 shakes her head, "No."

And why's that little girl? You don't want to live?

Victim #3's eyes water.

Victim #2 tries to hug her.

That goes against the rules.

You pull out the knife from her shoulder. Victim #2 is overcome with pain.

The other invaders react, wincing. Invader #2 chimes in, "Damn."

Victim #2 nearly passes out. You slap her across the face.

If you fall asleep, you'll never wake up.

So victims #2 and #3 sit side by side.

They don't beg for their life. Not until you become fed up with them, and they are told to lie down. Invaders surround them, two to a victim holding down one of their appendages.

Victim #2 starts, "Please…"

Victim #3 continues, "We'll do..."
Victim #2 finishes, "anything!"
Again she says, "Please, we'll do anything!"
You tell everyone to let go.
Really?

You force victim #2 to listen to victim #3 explain the "show" she watched on television.

In the daughter's words, the events that transpired over the past eighteen plus hours take on a frank, and far more demented spin.

The daughter's limited vocabulary for the would-be macabre results in a bluntness that causes the mother to cry out, "I'm sorry."

Victim #2 repeats her apology, "I'm sorry." With every repetition, she begins to drown out the daughter's summary of the events.

"I'm sorry. I'm sorry. I'm sorry. I'm sorry. I'm sorry. I'm sorry. I'm sorry. I'm sorry. I'm sorry. I'm sorry. I'm sorry. I'm sorry..."

But it's you that decides if she's sorry or not.

Another slap across the face. You look into her eyes.

You shake your head.

No you're not.

You point to the body of the husband and father, *He's the one that's sorry.*

There could be truth to this performance, the words being spoken, when really it's for the cults. It's more for the visceral gut reaction and carnage that is to be expected from these sorts of performances. It is never pretty. It is never anything more than alarming.

But it is entertaining.

Invader #5 hands out larger gloves, ones that go up to the elbows, and smocks. The fireproof gear came in handy after all.

Victim #2 is strapped down, invaders #2 and #4 holding her down.

You tell her, *Don't mind the gloves and the smocks. It's so no one is unharmed.*

You gesture for victim #3 to join you. *It's okay, sweetie you can stand up.*

What else is she going to do?

She follows your command.

When you tell her to pour the clear liquid from the white can all over her mother, she has no other recourse.

When you tell her to hold a piece of paper, perhaps from the pages of a book, the daughter holds onto it while you set flame to it with a torch lighter.

When you tell her to show it to her mother, the daughter shows her mother. She drops it when it burns her hand.

The paper falls to the floor, igniting the clear liquid.

For a few moments, invaders #2 and #4 hold onto victim #2's body.

When the flame engulfs her arms and legs, they let go.

Victim #2's body flails around on the ground. You hold up the gun, waiting until the last possible moment to return the scene to silence.

With the pull of the trigger, it returns to silence.

The only sound that can be heard is the sound of the flames burning bright.

"YOU DID THIS."

IT'S a smell you won't have to ever get used to, but give it a minute or so and you'll be able to work through it. The smell of burnt flesh has a way with sticking to surfaces. You won't have to worry about the smell leaving anytime before the authorities arrive.

Invader #2 shakes his head, "Shit, I didn't expect that to happen."

Invader #3 whispers, "It's not over yet."
But it's too late. It was recorded.

Invader #4 tends to the most important part of the performance: the aftermath. Sure, I tell you all about how the most important part is the casing. The most important part is the pulloff. The most important part is the spoilage. The most important part is that final scene. But I hope you're getting the point:
The most important part is the one you're currently in.

Invader #5 drenches the dead bodies in the flammable liquid.
He snaps his fingers, invader #3 tossing him the torch lighter.

He waits a moment, letting the piece of paper burn and curl, before setting fire to the bodies.

Everyone leaves the basement, following the camera's lead.

You sit on the couch, watching the television, directing where and what needs attention. No trace of the crew's DNA must remain. Now comes time for the chemical wash. One of invader #3's specialties is making sure the location is left clean.

No flecks of blood.

No spit.

Not so much as a piece of hair.

Though part of the risk, and the reward, is the jolt of worry and fear that comes with the impossible. It's impossible to leave the scene completely clean.

But you can try.

Some of the most successful performances end with the invaders imprisoned and publicly executed.

The camera sweeps through the crawlspace. Invader #5 is the one closest to vantage point #3 and so he goes through with the chemical wash, adding water to let it foam up for a deep clean.

The camera notes all the doorknobs. It's not just fingerprints —the gloves took care of that—but also the sweat.

You mustn't leave any bodily fluid behind.

The camera takes you to the dining room, a real problem area.

Invader #4 spends some time attempting to clean out the traces but, failing to do so, it is likely that the voice will become a suspect.

Worth laughing about this early out is how the authorities will follow that lead only to discover that the voice was one of the burnt bodies.

The camera skirts around the upstairs hallway, the blood

from invader #2's wound against the wall as well as your own in victim #4's room.

Invader #3 takes care of it.

The chemical wash does a good job of removing the trace even if it leaves behind its own imprint. When the authorities look around, they'll notice where you washed out potential evidence. It'll leave a mark. It usually lightens the color of a surface. Sometimes it causes the surface to change shades. In one drastic case, I've seen the wash burn through fabric and leave small craters in certain surfaces.

Despite the effects, everything is cosmetic.

Everything you choose to leave behind tells its share of the story.

Everything else is saved for the record, the one that'll leak from an anonymous source to all major media outlets. The way it's always been done.

The camera focuses on the exterior of the house, in particular the treehouse.

It's invader #4 who walks by the couch, "I'll take care of it."

She's outside in the dark of the night, flashlight in hand, picking up cigarette butts and the other objects left behind while in wait for the family's first move.

She doubles back, wherever footprints have been left, she muddies them up, clearing any and all tracks.

It must appear as though nothing on the outside has been disturbed; it must appear as though the incident occurred without any outside suspicion.

It happened.

And we don't know how...

The camera pans across various writing on the walls, mirrors, and other surfaces. But I don't think you'll have to worry about that. It'll add character. The more you leave behind pertaining to the actual performance, the more the authorities will begin processing this as much more than a robbery. I've seen performances that aimed high but cleaned all traces of their performance and the authorities figured it for a smash-and-grab break in that went awry, gunshots and all.

Curiosity is important.

You just want to make sure things are clean.

As clean as possible.

The camera captures the almost completely dark interior of the garage. Invader #5 walks downstairs, finishing up with everything upstairs.

He stops and watches.

He says, "I got it."

You sure?

Yeah.

Invader #4 doesn't return to the house; instead, she continues her search next door.

The camera follows her every step.

Inside the house, she pauses in the kitchen, trying to remember if she ate anything while they were there.

The camera doesn't tell and so she drags a large wastebin into the center of the kitchen and proceeds to shatter every plate, every single glass.

She has a lot of fun doing so and even goes out of her way to toss all the food too.

Invader #4 has time. She remains in the house, waiting for invader #5 to return.

After he finishes up with the garage, he heads back, walking into the kitchen right as invader #4 douses everything in the last bit of chemical wash she has left.

Invaders #4 and #5 nod at each other and proceed through the house, backtracking on their every move.

There's only one thing left. They head into the basement.

The camera captures the space right behind you.

Victim #3 stands there watching.

Has she been watching the entire time?

You leave her be. I still think it's a good idea.

It's risky but you've got to trust me.

You motion for her to sit down next to you, "Don't be shy."

The both of you watch the television.
Onscreen, it's you and her.
Perhaps there's nothing left.
We're getting to the end.

Invaders #2 and #3 walk back into the kitchen, gear collected. Premises clean.

Invaders #4 and #5 walk back inside the house a couple minutes later.

Victim #3 looks at you.
What is it?
She doesn't say anything. A blank expression.
You can tell me.
She blinks and then says, "You have a scary mask."
You laugh.
I laugh too. This is good.
Run with it.
Invader #2 says, "What about mine?"
He leans in, letting victim #3 have a look.
"Am I really fucking scary?"
She nods.
"Scarier than him?"
She shakes her head.
"We'll that's some bullshit," he stomps his foot down, wincing at the pain shooting up his wounded arm.
Invader #3 asks her, "Mine's not so bad, right?"
She takes a minute to look.
"Well? Not as bad as his right?"
She nods. Same blank expression.
There's laughter.
Invader #4 doesn't move, choosing to go last.
Invader #5 shrugs, and doesn't say a thing.
He kneels down in front of her.
She looks at him.
She looks at you.
The silence fills in the gaps between actions.
The daughter breathes out, "I'm hungry."

Because of his face?

She makes an exaggerated face, "No! I'm just hungry."

Invader #5 shrugs, "Guess I'm ranked at the bottom."

Invader #4 goes into the kitchen. She does what she did before, bowl, cereal, milk, but this time she adds something else, just enough to calm the young girl down.

Invader #4 walks up, handing the daughter the bowl.

"My favorite!"

But when she looks at invader #4, she moves away, leaning more in your direction. She closes her eyes.

You both trade glances.

Frightened?

Victim #3 nods, "He's scary."

He's scary.

It seems like the young girl has mixed up your faces. This is a good indication. The trauma of the situation has resulted in shock. The daughter's memory is jumbled. I won't say that it'll remain jumbled; there's a good chance that the events will line up at a later date in more of a logical manner. However, it does appear as though victim #3 is not processing the events in a clear manner.

Ask her.

Go ahead.

Ask her.

You might as well.

We should know.

You ask victim #3 about what happened. More so, you ask her about the summary she gave to her mother before the fire. You leave out the last part.

You don't want to unsettle the victim.

She sits back up.

She eats a spoonful of cereal.

Looks at you.

Stares at your face, the mask.

You ask again.

She swallows and then says, "My mom and my dad and and my pet dog and and and my brother they..."

Yes?

She eats another spoonful.

"They were killed by monsters?"

Monsters?

"Big monsters."

I see.

"Big monsters that talk like people."

Talk like people... now we're getting somewhere. Keep going.

What do they talk like?

She continues eating the cereal, "Umm, like my brother. They talk like they want to be right when, like mom says," victim #3 puts her hands on her hips, pretending to act like her mother in mid-rant, "he's probably wrong!"

I wonder if she meant the father and not the son.

No. It doesn't matter. Disregard.

They talk like people?

Victim #3 looks at the empty bowl of cereal, laps up a little bit of the milk, which, by now, has taken on the flavor of the cereal, "No. They talk like monsters that want to be people."

But they're monsters?

She nods, "Monsters. Big bad mean monsters."

A moment of silence and then she points at the television, "Like on TV!"

Does your mom let you watch those programs?

She grins, "No..." She blushes a little, giggles, "But I still watch them."

Shortly thereafter, victim #3 succumbs to the dosage, falling into a deep sleep. The rest of the crew descends into the basement.

It's almost dawn.

You might as well. That's a good call.

It'll be easier for her if she wakes up in her own bed.

You tell them, *I'll catch up.*

You carry the daughter in your arms up the stairs, past all the other bedrooms, setting her down in her own bed, blanket up to her chin. You look at her a moment and smile because you know that the camera captured it all.

You peek into the daughter's bedroom one last time before leaving to turn down the intercom in her room and her brother's, if only to keep her from waking when you leave.

Fast asleep, you marvel at her ability to cope with that's occurred.

But then when you don't understand what's happened and are told by others that it's a nightmare, perhaps the shock alone will carry you through to the next day.

Tomorrow, the daughter will discover the reality of the situation.

The authorities will discover a young child, the sole survivor, traumatized beyond belief. But I think it was better to keep her alive.

You could have ended it differently, but the daughter has a lot left to live for. It will take some time for her to recover. But not as long as many think.

There are plenty of survivors of the craft.

Victims that survived, yes.

It takes years to recover, but eventually you do.

And when you do. It's magical.

There's a whole world out there.

It opens itself up as if to welcome you in.

Just hope that it won't engulf you after you decide to take its embrace.

But that's the beauty, is it not?

We choose to believe in something even though it might be nothing.

The cults live and die by their beliefs.

Take off the masks, throw them in the fire, standing in a circle around the burning husk of bodies, the invaders take a final bow. By that, of course, I mean you share this one last moment before those roles are withdrawn.

Surrounding the pyre of bodies now more a melding of flesh, you know that there's only one thing left to do.

The invaders change into clean street clothes.

The outfits used are tossed into the fire too.

No one looks at each other's nakedness. The camera

captures the fire not the nude display. When the clothes are more a liquid goo, invaders #4 and #5 tend to the fire. It takes an extinguisher each before the fire is controlled.

Given that the room's fire alarms were disengaged, you couldn't just leave the house with the fire still burning. That would spread and burn the rest of the house down. You don't want the remnants of the performance to burn to the ground.

You want an innocent bystander. You want someone to discover the scene.

The aftermath. You don't want people in uniform, on the scene to tend to a fire.

Upstairs, invader #2 says something like, "Fuck the smell's already on these clothes."

Invader #4 sighs, "Change out of them when we're on the road."

Everyone's coming off of an adrenaline high.

The performance is finished.

One by one they step outside into the pre-dawn morning.

Good job. Finished, just in time.

Kind of funny, huh, how anticlimactic it feels after it's all over. That's how I felt too. For all the intensity, it ends with the same lull as the beginning, when you were casing. It ends with the same lull as after the second act. It ends with more of a pause, where you almost get a chance to look back and wonder how things would have been if you did it differently. That's the beauty of it, though. Because you know. No one else will. The cults won't ever know of the truest take. And neither will I.

I wasn't down there with you all.

I was a voice in your head.

I was the director, helping you fight through the dread.

You did this.

Now enjoy the consequences.

You are the last to leave the house. You stand there, letting it all sink in. And then you turn the music back on, the way you want the authorities to discover the aftermath.

Upstairs, a young child sleeps.

You look around the house, at the television that now shows white static.

And then you look into the camera.

You grab it, wiping the dirt from the lens.

And then you leave the same way you arrived.

CHAPTER
TWENTY-ONE

THE AUTHORITIES FIND the vehicle tracks first. A handful of phone calls from various hikers and other residents noted the vehicle as "seemingly abandoned" or "suspiciously parked." However, by the time the authorities responded to the disturbance, arriving near the southern entrance to a prominent private hiking trail, the vehicle had been moved.

Their findings were reported; which is to say, nothing was found.

Nothing but a few tire tracks.

Approximately a day after your departure, a landscaping crew arrived to tend to the exterior of the house. The daughter watched from her window, tapping on the glass, hoping they'd hear her. She'd tell the authorities later that she was too afraid to leave her bedroom.

"There are monsters."

The detective would deny her claims, doing her best to console the child, "They were people. Bad people. Nothing more."

But the landscapers couldn't hear the daughter over the noise of their mowers and hedgers. Despite phone calls and knocks on the door, the daughter couldn't leave her room. They heard the music but didn't think much of it.

They were more annoyed by the perceived rudeness of the mother.

For years, they've tended to the family's estate. For years, it was the mother that opened the door and acted politely enough before tending to the day's bill and confirmation of the previously planned schedule.

On that day, there was no response. Despite repeated ringing of the doorbell and calls, there was nothing that could be done. They marked the account delinquent and continued to the next work order. There didn't seem to be any problem. Who would really consider loud music a warning sign?

When the husband didn't report to work, few noticed. Sick maybe. Hungover more likely. The typical excuses were applied.

Similar expected excuses for both son and daughter.

Schools left messages on the mother and father's cellphones.

The pattern continued:

Silence around the house, the family noted as missing in their lives.

The mother's online activity dropped off severely. Though a few users noticed a lack of reply to her messages, life continued.

The same went for both kids.

It was on a Wednesday, when one of the husband's mistresses, not yet someone he'd slept with but more of an acquaintance, a secretary of another architect, a friend, one that had made plans with the husband to meet that Monday, the Monday that had passed. Despite numerous voicemail messages and emails, the secretary did not receive a response. It wasn't until she called up mutual friends, those that would have spoken with the husband on more of a daily basis, that she suspected something may have happened. Going against her instincts, she drove to the house.

She peeked through the closed gate.

She climbed the gate.

She walked around the house.

She heard the music.

She heard the knocking on the window.

She saw the daughter.

After a wave, the daughter made a panicked gesture.

Something was clearly wrong. The secretary could feel it.

She called 911 but chose to remain anonymous.

She ran back to her car and parked a block away, waiting for the authorities to arrive. When the authorities arrived, it was a single squad car. Unlike the secretary, they didn't have reason to climb over the gate. They stood there, inspecting the house from a far-off angle.

One said to the other, "What do you want to do?"

The other thought about it and then said, "It doesn't look like there's a problem."

Irritated and afraid that the officers would give up and drive away, the secretary walked over, telling them that she had been the caller. She told them what she saw.

"Are you positive that's what you saw, ma'am?"

"Yes", she replied, "and don't call me ma'am. I'm not that old."

The officers helped each other over the gate.

One of the officers stopped her, "You better stay here."

From her vantage point, which invader #1 had used to survey the home from a distance, she watched as the officers disappeared around the house.

Minutes passed before one of the officers could be seen running back around toward the front door. The officer said something into a receiver attached to his right shoulder. After a brief exchange, the officer tried the door.

It was unlocked. No one had tried the doorknob.

The music flooded out. You could hear it from the gate.

Moments later the officer ran back out, the other officer joining him. They returned to the gate, one officer busy calling dispatch, the other ushering the secretary back to her vehicle.

"Please, you have to leave."

"Why? Just tell me why?"

Please, ma'am."

The secretary frowned, "What? What happened?"

"This is a crime scene. You do not belong here."

The media picked up on the story. Across hundreds of outlets, associated and independent, national and international, the talk surrounding the invasion was the same: monsters. The daughter became the focal point of the media, perhaps due to the sheer fact that she had survived three and a half days without food or water. Perhaps it had to do with the fact that she survived at all. It's rare for "events of this magnitude" to have any survivors, much less a young child.

Perhaps it was her version of the events that caused the most concern.

"They were monsters."

The line echoed across social media.

Stories, both fact and fiction, appeared from all channels.

The media had picked up on the invasion.

And this was long before the leak.

The authorities undersell what they discovered in the neighboring house fourteen hours into their investigation, opting instead to keep the story as straight as possible.

The media doesn't focus on the second family.

The media focuses on the little girl.

The media focuses on the burned bodies.

The media focuses on the family's story, a typical upper middle class suburban story, right down to the paper trail left behind by its members.

The son becomes a suspect early in the case due to the conversations recovered from his social media accounts and subsequently published across the associated press.

This story doesn't hold if only because the son had been one of the victims.

The voice's DNA is found. It takes approximately a week before any information pertaining to the name and the probable suspect's whereabouts are recovered.

During that time, the little girl becomes a bit of an internet meme.

Exaggerations of the invasion spread across message boards.

Creepypasta, otherwise known by the cults as online-horror fan fiction, leaks and manages to reach the detectives working the case.

One particular piece of fiction incriminates the detective.

The detective reacts harshly. After a falling out due to negative public response, the detective is quietly reassigned to another department.

The voice's name is given to the media by an insider source close to the investigation. Approximately twelve hours later, via official report from those in charge of the case, the voice is declared dead. He had been one of the burnt bodies.

Without any clear leads, the authorities continue to piece together a puzzle that cannot be completed, not without the sample.

The sample is leaked via anonymous sources to five independent media outlets.

Twenty-four hours later, studios begin solicitations.

There's a need to know more, given that the sample provided is an eighth of the material captured on record. This is where you shine because you get to walk into a coffee shop or restaurant and hear about the invasion without any worry of there being suspicion.

You get to sit down at a table in the back, one reserved for you, and there's a man in a suit waiting to shake your hand.

You both know but there's no worry.

The man isn't trying to solve the case.

The man is a businessman and, what's more, he's a member too.

Perhaps he's performed one with less interest, but he has an appreciation for the craft and that's all that matters.

You shake his hand and sit down.

This isn't the first meeting you've had. It's the fifth, perhaps the sixth, in what will be approximately a dozen offers. A bidding war between who gets to know the truth.

The one that owns the truth holds the rights to how the truth is spun.

Now that's entertainment.

The man does his best and, honestly, his offer is one of the better ones.

The man discusses the business, the fickleness of the cults, and, more importantly, the culture that contains them:

"Everyone's looking to make it big. Killing a person isn't enough. You had to do it in sheer brutality. Then it was sheer creativity. Now it's both, but something else too. What is it? No one knows—that's the beauty of it: The next in a series of parables on how to be a part of a shooting star, the latest craze."

The man grins, "No home is safe. No home is ever safe. No building is really secure. Nothing is safe because everyone that wants to be famous is looking for the same thing. They want to feel again."

You meet with the other studio executives but the man with the proclamation bids the most and therefore wins the rights to the truth.

The record is submitted to the studio via an encrypted private download. Attached to the .avi are three documents with details, commentary, and cast.

The studio begins work on a script.

They hire three scriptwriters but after two weeks, fire all but one.

The media receives portions of the full record, but only because the studio used their correspondents to create more buzz for the invasion.

Not that there needed to be any additional buzz.

You stick around, often receiving more information about the inner workings of various projects to be made based on your performance. However, I know how it feels.

It feels underwhelming, like the best part is over.

I understand. We talk about it a lot. Hours on the phone.

About an hour in, we get right to it.

There's talk about sequels... but that's the studio white noise getting to you. They want more of the same if only because "the same" is currently buzzworthy.

But we talk about it, the irony that is the truth.

And you get to a point where it makes sense.

It's the fear that gets them. When it gets old, fear disappears.

If you want more, you'll have to perform.

I ask you—

What's your motivation?

During some calls you don't know.

And others you reveal information about another performance, one you've been thinking about in broad strokes. I'm quick to encourage the concept, understanding that you will return with more experience. You'll want another director, someone that can add rather than fix, present alternate ideas rather than lecture. But then again, that's bound to happen. It happened with me and it'll happen with you. No hard feelings.

What's your motivation?

If you have to take a moment to guess, you shouldn't go through with it.

It feels like it was only yesterday when you met with the studio executive but today is the day you get a pre-release screening of your performance.

The studio went all-out on the production.

You sit in the small but luxurious in-house theater alongside the rest of the executives and a few celebrity journalists.

Somewhere in the back of the theater the actor that played your role, invader #1, slouches in a chair, perhaps nervous but most likely disinterested.

The film begins and ends without a single thought coming to mind.

Afterward, the executives and journalists approve, a mixture of excitement and relief permeates throughout the room.

They ask you for your thoughts and you choose to embellish them.

You lean towards the positive, if only because it's easier to agree with everybody than criticize the adaptation.

You don't know what to think.

It doesn't look like the performance.

But you see, it isn't your performance.

Your experiences will never match theirs. What the world will see is filtered through a number of lenses, a number of minds, when it is you that saw what the camera saw during first recording.

When the adaptation premieres nationwide, it is a resounding success.

But you feel nothing.

You feel as though it was a box office bust.

Despite the hype and the cults clamoring over various theories, you have moved on. It doesn't feel the same, does it?

You think about contacting the other invaders, but you never gain enough energy to actually pick up the phone and call.

Most of the time, you watch other peoples' performances.

You begin to appreciate the leaked records you find of full performances, including mine. You become like everyone else, the cults of the rural curiosities, searching for the source to their fears in the prepackaged consumerism of popular culture.

The daughter is a featured guest at the premiere, pictures of her smiling and waving at the camera. The daughter receives a fair bit of publicity. She becomes a celebrity.

There's talk of her being in other projects.

There's a lot of talk about her overcoming such a horrible tragedy.

Horrible tragedy, as a term, is thrown around as often as "successful" is desired by longtime members of the cults, the ones itching for a vantage point of their own.

What's your motivation?

Every one of us asks ourselves that question, over and over again.

I'm not going to ask you to reply. We've been through this over and over again. You'll recover what you've lost. If you find reason to once again perform, you'll see that it'll just fall into your lap. It'll fuel the best of your days while helping you through the worst of them. Until then, hold onto that question.

Never stop asking yourself that question.

Whatever the answer, make sure to save it for yourself.

Perhaps one night, or maybe it's a dull Saturday afternoon

full of early sips of a drink while filling the hours until there's something else to do, it breaks.

Whatever it is, it breaks and finally lets you go.

It's the same thing every invader fights in the aftermath of their performance. Think of it as a high or a low, a sense of euphoria or a dire episode of depression. Whatever it is, it's the emotional impact that trails behind.

It's the shellshock of our times.

The sense of emptiness after such a profound high is dealt with by invaders in different ways. But eventually it breaks. You move on.

Whether or not you choose, once again, to perform, you accept that you're the same as everyone else, the cults watching as much as criticizing.

You reach for the camera, pointing it at your face, looking right into it, the lens a few inches from your face. And you speak. You begin to fill in their answers, wise to the usual responses. You picture yourself in a position that had once been out of reach. You wait for someone to contact you, asking for advice. You wait, never losing interest.

Because, you see... the wait, it won't be long.

A QUERY FOR THE CULTS

TO WHOM IT MAY CONCERN—

So you were here, and you were watching, so what do you think? Really now?

If it was too much, what kept you from looking away?

Why did you watch the rest of it?

What must that imply? As yet another of the cults, do you fancy yourself against it yet captivated, or against it and curious?

If the latter, are you looking for advice? A mentor?

I have a lot of experience and I've directed more than a few. It's only a matter of time before armchair ranting and hating becomes legitimate curiosity. And when that time comes, you'll be like the cops, the investigators, you'll be right there sneaking in for a look, and more so to be there, in the thick of a performance. Then you'll wonder. But I'll tell you, there are a number of people involved, far more than the ones named and/or mentioned in the media, within a performance. Like any craft, it seeks to consume you.

What I ask is, quite simply, do you feel as though you might be consumed?

What about the camera?

What about it? It's everywhere.

If it exists, the camera's going to catch it.

Anything else is your word against mine.

You gotta admit: You were entertained.

ACKNOWLEDGMENTS

A writer finds a way to write the book, but they need more than that to give the book life. It takes a network of trusted friends and colleagues. Thank you, Christoph Paul, Leza Cantoral, Sarah Miniaci, Janice Lee, John Maher, Cynthia Pelayo, Eric LaRocca, Joshua Hull, Nick Antosca, Rob Hart, Sadie Hartmann, Dan Chaon, Rachel Harrison, Kathy Koja, Brian Evenson, B.R. Yeager, Brian Asman, Lane Heymont, Nat Cassidy, Dan Powell, my parents, my sister, my family, and everyone that gives a shit about anything I wrote or will ever write.

ABOUT THE AUTHOR

Michael J. Seidlinger is a Filipino American author of *Anybody Home?* (CLASH Books, 2022), *Scream* (Bloomsbury's Object Lessons series), and other books. He has written for, among others, *Wired, Buzzfeed, Thrillist, Goodreads, The Observer, Polygon, The Believer,* and *Publishers Weekly.* He teaches at Portland State University and has led workshops at Catapult, Kettle Pond Writer's Conference, and Sarah Lawrence. You can find him online on Twitter (@mjseidlinger) and Instagram @michaelseidlinger.

ALSO BY MICHAEL J. SEIDLINGER

FICTION

Dreams of Being

My Pet Serial Killer

Falter Kingdom

The Strangest

Messes of Men

The Face of Any Other

Mother of a Machine Gun

The Fun We've Had

The Laughter of Strangers

The Sky Conducting

NONFICTION

Scream (Object Lessons)

Runaways: A Writer's Dilemma

Mark Z. Danielewski's House of Leaves: *Bookmarked*

POETRY

Standard Loneliness Package

ALSO BY CLASH BOOKS

I'M FROM NOWHERE

Lindsay Lerman

THE PAIN EATER

Kyle Muntz

NIGHTMARES IN ECSTACY

Brendan Vidito

DIMENTIA

Russell Coy

SILVERFISH

Rone Shavers

HEXIS

Charlene Elsby

COMAVILLE

Kevin Bigley

CHARCOAL

Garrett Cook

PEST

Michael Cisco

HIGH SCHOOL ROMANCE

Marston Hefner

PROXIMITY

Sam Heaps

WE PUT THE LIT IN LITERARY

CLASHBOOKS.COM

FOLLOW US

FB

TWITTER

IG

@clashbooks

PUBLICIST FOR MICHAEL J. SEIDLINGER

Sarah Miniaci PR

sarah@sarahminiacipr.com

CPSIA information can be obtained
at www.ICGtesting.com
Printed in the USA
JSHW021821060922
30096JS00002B/2